The Ravenmaster's Revenge

The Return of King Arthur

Jacob Sannox

Cover by BetiBup33 - https://twitter.com/BetiBup33

Typeset by Polgarus Studio – www.polgarusstudio.com

Thank you for reading The Ravenmaster's Revenge: The Return of King Arthur.

I would love to keep you updated about my new releases, so if you would like to hear more about my work, please consider signing up for my Readers' Club at www.jacobsannox.com.

I'll also be running giveaways for my members.

It would be fantastic (and much appreciated) if you would leave me a review wherever you bought or downloaded your copy, as it's one of the best ways for new readers to find out that my books exist.

I look forward to hearing from you!

Jacob Sannox

'You profess to love your country, but what does that mean? Do you love the land, its ruler or its people? To honour all three at once is often no mean feat.'
- Captain Arthur Grimwood

Acknowledgements

Thanks to Mum, Dad, Anna and Sami for being my first readers!

Chapter One

September 2019
The Tower of London, England

Six ravens stood in a row upon the lawn. An unkindness.

They stood still with their backs to the river, facing the White Tower. It was as though the birds could see through the stone wall and into the building, focusing on some unknown point.

Their keeper, the Ravenmaster of the Tower, tried to engage with them, but they ignored him and ate nothing, even when he tried to bribe them with blood biscuits.

The Tower was open to visitors, and the ravens drew more than their fair share of attention on that chilly Wednesday morning. Schoolchildren on trips asked their teachers why the ravens weren't moving, and if they were even real. Adults speculated about the cause of the birds' strange behaviour, and, more towards the end of the day, as the light failed, a sense of disquiet fell upon the Tower.

'Legend goes that if the ravens leave the Tower, first the White Tower then England will fall,' was heard in various forms, thousands of times that day.

The ravens watched and waited.

The time came for them to return to their aviaries, and for the first time during his six years in the job, the Ravenmaster felt perturbed by his charges and feared how they would react to him when he approached. Yet he need not have worried. They hopped quietly onto his glove one at a time and allowed themselves to be carried home, never taking their eyes from the Tower. The first raven sat upon its perch in silence and continued its vigil, and, one at a time, the Ravenmaster carried the birds home, each one joining its companions in staring up at the White Tower.

Silent and taking no food, the ravens looked up at the White Tower.

Branok, the true Ravenmaster, was awake again.

September 2019
Hertfordshire, England

The children had died instantly.

Carol never regained consciousness but the hospital kept her alive for a few days. David felt as though his wife had slipped from a ledge and he'd caught her by the fingertips. Frantic, desperate moments ensued during which his hopes for Carol's survival defied the certain reality that, inevitably, she'd fall.

She fell.

The last time they all spoke was a typical Wednesday morning. David got up later than he should have and skipped breakfast so that Peter and Alice could have theirs.

Carol and David got the children ready with only minimal bickering then, pausing to give his wife the briefest of pecks on the cheek, David hurried them out of the house and into the car, still just about on track for the school run before work.

Carol picked Peter and Alice up at the end of the day and her car was the last to join a queue in the nearside lane of the M1 on the way home.

Carol had been stuck in traffic, reading messages scrawled in the dirt on the filthy rear doors of a van while the children chatted in the back, when Simon Renfrew, texting while he drove, failed to notice that the vehicles in front had stopped.

The lorry didn't so much hit the car as flatten it.

David never went home during the period Carol was in hospital. He finally returned on the day she died, but on arrival, he looked upon the house with new eyes.

The curtains were still drawn upstairs in the front bedrooms, the children's bedrooms. David stood in the street, leaning on the gatepost and looking over the driveway towards the living-room window. He could just make out the grandfather clock and the dining table.

Before him, the last moments his family had spent together were preserved. The bad news had not been through the gate, had not walked the path or unlocked the door. The tragedy had not packed up Peter's cars or Alice's crayons from their bedroom floors. The plates on the draining board had yet to be informed of the loss. Carol's half-finished coffee would be waiting patiently for her return, just where she had left it on top of the piano, leaving a ring on the varnish.

The Bolton family's life was waiting for them. And if he turned the key and let in the air from a world in which his wife and children were dead, if he crossed that threshold?

David's keys sat on his open palm, and he held them up, scrutinising them. He returned them to his trouser pocket and walked away from the house, from his Pompeii.

Chapter Two

England – The Fifth Century A.D.

'It's true, sire,' said Sir Tristan as he gathered his breath. He dropped to one knee and bowed his head before the king in the dim candlelit tent. 'Mordred's army has made camp at Camlann.'

'We must meet him far sooner than I anticipated,' brooded Arthur.

A small cough behind him. Merlin stepped up to his side. Arthur cocked his head, and Merlin leant in to whisper.

'Aye, true enough,' said Arthur. 'But if we move against him now, perhaps we can catch him unawares.'

Arthur stood, a towering figure in brown, boiled leather armour over a mail shirt, and with a silver circlet upon his brow, his beard streaked with grey.

'Sir Tristan, pass the word to all of my knights. We march as soon as we can strike camp,' said Arthur. Sir Tristan bowed and backed out of the tent.

'I fear this will go ill, boy. Why do you never listen?' said Merlin, gripping his staff.

Arthur squeezed the wizard's upper arm in a comforting gesture and smiled down at him, looking into his ancient grey eyes.

'I cannot forever err on the side of caution, hiding behind my palisades, Merlin. Mordred means to bring us to battle, and it is now inevitable. We will make an account of ourselves, however we may fare in the end,' said Arthur. He drew Excalibur and examined the blade.

'I can only hope I need not kill Mordred to end the fighting,' he said, and the wizard could hear the strain in the king's voice. 'Perhaps he will listen to reason.'

'I hope so. It would be an evil deed for a father to shed the blood of a son, but then no less than it is for a son to shed the blood of his father,' said Merlin.

'Your advice is of use, as always,' Arthur laughed, and muttering, Merlin headed out into the night, leaving the king to his own counsel.

Arthur fastened his cloak about his shoulders and stepped out into the chill night air. His army was arrayed before him, thousands strong and waiting. Arthur's squire held the reins to his charger, and the king thanked him as he mounted.

He spurred the animal into a trot and rode down the line of his knights, acknowledging each of them in turn.

Tristan, Agravain, Bedivere, Gareth, Kay, Percival, Lamorak, Galahad, Gaheris, Dagonet, Bors, Lucan, Ector, Geraint and Gawain.

They rode out together at the head of a great column, which snaked across the moors behind them, trampling the grass into the mud. Tristan rode on his right, and Merlin on his left.

On through the night rode Arthur, Merlin and the knights.

Arthur spurred his charger into a gallop, and his army burst forth from the treeline and rampaged down the slope towards Mordred's camp, before which his army was only now assembling, caught unawares as they were.

Hooves thundered, and the ground shook as Arthur drew Excalibur then held it aloft. His knights rode in a line beside him, and his infantry roared as they charged.

They would break Mordred's forces with this charge, thought Arthur, smashing apart whatever passed for a line in the dim light before the dawn. The king and his knights galloped toward the scantly armoured men who were forming up before them, brandishing weapons and cowering behind shields, no doubt aware that they would shortly be trampled underfoot.

'Cavalry, sire!' called Gawain, and when Arthur looked off to his left, he saw a large number of horsemen charging at their flank. Mordred's banner flew above them.

But it was too late, Arthur was committed and as his knights rode down the first of Mordred's men, so too did Mordred ride over Arthur's unprotected foot soldiers.

'For Briton!' roared Arthur as he brought down Excalibur, cleaving an opposing Briton's head in two. 'For Briton!'

First one man then another fell beneath his sword strokes and then someone hacked through his charger's leg. The horse let out a terrible cry as it fell, and Arthur crashed to the ground.

He was up again in mere seconds. Arthur unleashed a flurry of blows, driving back the men who stood to face him, felling them one by one. He wheeled and parried, stabbed and slashed. None could stand before him. Mordred's soldiers hesitated, giving him space, and Arthur pulled off his helm so he could look directly into their eyes.

They wavered in the king's presence and under his gaze.

'Hear me!' Arthur roared. 'You follow a false sovereign, who desires naught but power. Hear now the voice of the true king. I pardon your sins, brothers, and call on you now to aid me in throwing down my son, born of treachery. Rise up, my Britons! Take Mordred alive!'

All those who listened truly heard him. It mattered not what Arthur said, but his voice itself carried a power, imbued with a certainty and steadfast nobility that struck the hearts of those who heard it. Arthur beseeched and ensnared them, and they rallied to him, joining his cause.

The battle raged on.

The morning sun was up when finally both Arthur found Mordred, and Mordred found Arthur upon the field of battle.

The dead and dying lay all around, both armies now depleted to mere companies of men. Only Tristan and Agravain remained by Arthur's side, and the three men worked closely together, watching over one another and driving their enemies back with both their swordsmanship and their determination. Until, that is, they met Mordred's household guard, who were clad in iron, and were as disciplined a fighting force as ever Arthur had seen.

They withstood Arthur's assault, and suddenly he and his company found they were hard-pressed to stand their ground. Mordred's guard swarmed all around them, and Arthur found that he fought alone on a bare hill, surrounded by his foes.

He fought on, though his muscles cried out, and he bled from a multitude of wounds, his face bruised and his hair matted with blood. Blow after blow he dealt his enemies, but ever they came on at him, the circle closing in, like wolves surrounding their prey.

Arthur felled them one by one, growing ever more exhausted, until finally he saw his son standing before him, shield in his left hand and sword in his right, the blade resting against his shoulder.

Arthur paused, gathering his wits and what was left of his strength.

'Put an end to this, Mordred,' he rasped. 'Lay down your arms.'

Mordred grinned back at Arthur as the guard closed around them.

A sudden commotion drew Arthur's attention as Tristan launched an assault from the left, yet his knight could not break through. Mordred engaged Tristan, and he was forced back. Arthur looked away, knowing that he was in great peril, standing there before his son, who was a product of intrigue and incest.

Where is Merlin?

Arthur stood alone, and Merlin did not come.

Mordred raised his shield and took a lazy practice swing with his sword.

Arthur adjusted his stance, raising Excalibur into a high guard, but hoping it would not come to a fight.

'I will pardon you and your men, if you will unite with us again,' said Arthur.

'There is only room on the throne for one man, Father,' said Mordred, and he pointed his sword at Arthur's head. 'And only one crown.'

With that Mordred burst forward. Arthur stepped aside, and Mordred struck out with his shield. Arthur checked the blow with Excalibur's cross-guard and staggered as Mordred aimed a wicked slash at his face.

Arthur stepped back and parried as Mordred slashed at his head. Excalibur cut through the iron blade as though it were cutting through air. Mordred staggered back.

Arthur heard Tristan roaring and Agravain calling his name. Once more Mordred's men were drawn off to combat the onslaught of his most fearsome knights.

One of Mordred's men threw his master a mace, and the second it was in his hand, Arthur's son charged again, this time running forward with his shield held high.

Excalibur's tip burst through the shield as Arthur toppled back into the mud, and Mordred landed atop him. The mace landed beside Arthur's head, splattering his face with mud. Arthur hauled at Excalibur, trying to work the blade free, and as he did so, slicing through the shield, blood flicked out, following the arc of the blade.

It took Arthur a moment to realise that he must have stabbed Mordred through the shield. And then he cried out, struggling for breath as something thumped repeatedly into his side, over and over and over. Arthur cried out and threw back his head, tossing the silver circlet to the ground.

Men hauled Mordred to his feet, and Arthur saw not only that his son was mortally wounded – Excalibur had rent a great gash through his guts – but that he held a bloody knife in his right hand. Arthur fought to breathe, gasping in the mud as Mordred contorted, crying out. He slumped, but his men held him up and Mordred caught his father's eye. He stared at Arthur for a second until all life went out of him.

Finally Tristan stepped into view, hacking down the men who had steadied Mordred. Arthur lay back and closed his eyes, as a booted foot crunched into his skull and yet another stamped down on his right hand, its fingers still clutching Excalibur. He felt himself beginning to fade, felt a heavy, dreary sleep coming upon him as pain lanced through his side.

And there upon the field of Camlann, Arthur, King of the Britons, began to slip from the world to the sound of Tristan's anguished cries and battle coming to an end.

Tristan and Agravain stood over Arthur, killing any who dared approach to defile him. When Percival and then Gawain found them, they carried their king from the field while the last of the fighting drew to a close and, both sides leaderless, neither victorious, the armies began to wander away. The moaning of the injured and calls of soldiers looking for fallen friends accompanied the knights as they carried Arthur, bearing him away into the woodland atop the slope. There they laid him upon Tristan's cloak.

Merlin appeared from the trees and moved slowly and silently to Arthur's side, hands shaking.

He knelt by the king's battered head and wiped blood from Arthur's face with the hem of his long robe as the knights gathered in a circle around their fallen leader.

Merlin cradled Arthur's face, closed his eyes as Arthur drew his last breath and began to speak in an ancient tongue. The woods shuddered and leaves fell all about them as Merlin fell silent, the rite completed.

'Is there nothing that can be done, Merlin?' asked Agravain, and the wizard looked up, fury in his eyes.

'No, nothing can be done. To think of all that should have been achieved!' he spat, but in an instant his angry words turned to tears. He spoke through them, and the gathered knights leant in closer to hear what he had to say.

'He will return when we have greatest need of him. His spirit is bound to these lands, and his body is preserved.'

And they gasped as they saw that it was so. Arthur's wounds healed, and he appeared to be sleeping.

Merlin stood and addressed them.

'He will have need of you again,' he said, his voice grave. 'Will you hold to your oaths and go with him into the long dark, awaiting the day when you are called back to serve him once more?'

'I hold to my oath,' said Tristan.

'As do I,' said Agravain, and one by one the others echoed the promise.

'Then let it be so. We will bear him away to a

place where he may rest, and you can lie beside him until the time comes.'

Merlin pulled a pouch from within his robe and tossed it to Tristan.

'A sprinkle into wine, and you will join him,' said Merlin. The knight nodded that he understood.

And so King Arthur, the man, passed away, and over time, the story of his life became embellished into legend, and history forgot him.

Chapter Three

October 2019

Arthur cradled the steaming mug before him, and once more lifted it to sip. A brief, sharp pain on his lips and the tiniest drop of black coffee, tasting of cigarette ash, reached his tongue. He set the mug back down on the plastic table cover, leaning on his forearms and savouring the warmth through the wool of his fingerless gloves, and the urgent heat on his bare fingertips.

He kept his eyes on the old man queuing at the counter. He'd barely changed at all since last they'd seen one another, a long, long time ago, his long grey beard, his whiter hair tied back into a pony tail, which hung down to his waist. The old man wore a faded shirt with yellow patches under the arms. Baggy, brown corduroy trousers hung low thanks to a broken leather belt, held together – just – by a safety pin. Arthur could see that the old man wore another pair of trousers underneath. His skin was dirty, and not a hard day's work kind of grubbiness. This was the deeply ingrained unwashed sort, which blackened his pores. Two tables back, Arthur was too far away to smell the man, but the odour rising from his coat, thrown over the back of the chair opposite him, pockets bulging, was redolent of many unwashed weeks, if not months, of urine, body odour and alcohol. The old man was not out of place amongst the ragtag clientele of the café, and no one reacted to him, not so much as leaving him a little space in the queue.

Arthur stood out in that place, surrounded by life's waifs and strays, Seventies décor, the scent of eggs swimming in oil, and the sound of blown noses and coughing. His neatly trimmed beard, suit coat, starched shirt, polished shoes and composed, confident demeanour were incongruous.

Finally, the large woman in the chequered blue tabard at the till took the old man's order, screeched it back to the harried, skinny boy working the grill. The old man strolled back to the table with an ease belying his age. He dropped down opposite Arthur, who managed not to grimace as the stench redoubled.

The old man sighed and sat back in his chair, smiling and rubbing his filthy hands together.

'Just wait, Arthur, just wait,' he said, his every word a promise, knowing eyebrow arched.

'Good?' said Arthur.

'Doesn't cover it, boy. Just wait,' said the old man.

And they did. Arthur's coffee finally reached the ideal temperature, just a little too hot, and he kept the mug under his nose between sips. The coffee was bad, but its aroma was definitely preferable to the others nearby.

'Where have you been?' asked Arthur. 'It's been, what, seventy years?'

'Seventy-four,' said the old man. 'And just anywhere you'd expect me to be. I spent as much time in London as I could bear, but I can do no good there. Look at me, Arthur. I've been ushered away from Westminster with a flea in my ear at least three times.'

'They do say "dress for the job you want",' said Arthur, and his face betrayed a smile, but the old man frowned.

They said nothing more until the food arrived, plates set down with a thump, chinking against the napkin-swaddled cutlery.

Arthur winced as the old man made a pincer motion, snatched up a rasher of bacon between his filthy fingers and sandwiched it between two triangular pieces of toasted white bread. The old man was too fixated on his food to notice the younger man's reaction, and Arthur watched him fondly, warmth kindling in his heart at seeing the old man once more.

Arthur tucked in too, and by God, the old man was right. The two men made inroads across their plates with military efficiency, working in silence, consuming and savouring in a comfortable silence. Fork and knife clashed, bean juice dripped and was promptly swabbed up. Stab, cut, devour.

The battle of breakfast drew to a close, and none remained standing on the field.

The old man unfurled his napkin and dabbed around his moustache and chin, and Arthur did the same. He returned to his coffee and, satisfied, sat back with one elbow resting on the back of the chair beside him.

'Your judgment is as honed as it ever was,' Arthur

conceded then raised his fist to his mouth to disguise a small burp.

'You doubted it?' snapped the old man. 'I told you, boy. There was a time when you heeded my words.'

'Frequently, but never consistently,' said Arthur.

'Impetuous fool,' the old man grumbled.

Arthur stood, picking up his cane, but the old man caught his wrist.

'Where are you going?'

'To relieve myself,' said Arthur, 'if you must know.'

The old man nodded and released his grip.

'I thought you were about to pay,' he confessed, then, straightening up, he added without making eye contact, 'And why not? Go ahead, boy.'

Arthur declined to mention that he had made no such offer, but paid on the way back from the toilet nonetheless. *And why not*, he thought? He owed the old man enough.

'I live nearby,' said Arthur, returning to the table.

'I am well aware, thank you,' said the old man. 'Lay on, Macduff.'

Arthur called his driver while the old man was pulling on his coat.

'Absolutely not,' said the old man. 'You should be ashamed.'

Arthur was prepared.

'It's electric. And you'd prefer we walk? It's a good ten miles, home,' said Arthur.

The old man shrugged the coat over his shoulders.

'Nearer eight, I think you'll find. And yes, I'd walk rather than spout any more poison into the air.'

And yet you arranged to meet here, thought Arthur, but he held his tongue.

The sleek silver sedan pulled up at the kerbside, and Arthur ushered the old man out of the café ahead of him. Windswept leaves of gold and brown drifted all around, and Arthur felt their fallen brothers crunch beneath his feet as he crossed the pavement, limping and leaning on his cane.

His driver, fully decked-out in a Savile Row suit and cap, opened the door and without acknowledging him, the old man disappeared into the rear seat.

'Thank you, Gareth,' said Arthur as he climbed in, too.

The drive to Arthur's home took no more than half an hour. To begin with, the old man stared out of the window and harrumphed whenever he saw something or someone that displeased him, but once they were clear of the traffic at the centre of town, the houses and shops gave way to hedgerows, hemming in fields, and bare hillsides in the middle distance. The old man fell silent, content to simply watch the world go by. Arthur eyed the old man up and down, reviewing the state of his clothing once more. He schemed.

Before long the winding road passed through woodland and the car turned into a short drive barred by gates that prevented access to Arthur's walled estate. They swung open, and the car passed through. Arthur heard the old man grumble something under his breath.

'Thank you. I like it,' said Arthur, and the old man harrumphed without turning to look.

Gareth parked the car before the front door in the shade of an old oak that stood at the centre of the courtyard. The old man stood looking up at it, nodding, before he followed Arthur to the door, where they were met by a pair of suited men.

'Good morning, sir,' they said in unison.

'Morning, Tristan,' Arthur replied. 'Would you be so good as to ask the kitchen to send a pot of coffee to me in the drawing room?'

'Very good, sir,' replied Tristan, bowing his head.

The other man closed the door behind them and, Arthur noted, he offered to take the old man's wretched coat without hesitation. The old man shrugged him off, removed his coat and handed it to the suited man then looked him up and down.

'What have you been reduced to?' he snapped.

'I am ever his humble servant, Merlin,' replied the man through gritted teeth.

'Servant is right,' muttered the old man.

'Percival, please run our guest a bath,' said Arthur, causing the old man to turn and glare at him, but Arthur raised a hand.

'No arguments,' said Arthur, and, still grumbling, the old man allowed Percival to show him up the broad staircase before them, turning up the smaller set of steps to the left when they reached the top.

When he was sure they were out of earshot, Arthur turned back to Tristan.

'While he's bathing, retrieve his clothes, get his sizes, and send Gareth out to replace them, will you?'

Tristan grinned.

'Something amusing?' asked Arthur.

'All the trials we have faced together, and yet you send me alone to complete the most perilous task, sir?'

'We all must prove our worth,' laughed Arthur. 'I suggest holding your breath.'

'Duly noted, sir. I'll see to your coffee first, in case I meet my demise in the attempt.'

Chapter Four

19th of January 1486
The Second Year of the Reign of
King Henry VII of the House of Tudor

'It is done,' said Merlin to the boy as he opened his eyes. The boy yawned and stretched, rubbing sleep from his eyes.

The wizard knelt within the stone circle of Stonehenge, the boy sitting cross-legged before him.

'Do you see?' Merlin asked. The boy cocked his head to one side. The wizard sighed and, reaching out, rapped the boy's forehead with his knuckles.

'The marriage is complete, Branok. The wedding night has passed,' Merlin snapped.

'King Henry VII of the House of Lancaster has married Elizabeth of the House of York,' Merlin prompted. 'And what does this mean?'

Branok rubbed at the sore spot on his forehead and chewed at his lower lip. Finally, he spoke.

'The white rose and red rose are united, Merlin,' said Branok, hesitantly. He drew back a little, as though expecting to be swiped, but Merlin nodded, smiling.

'Good, good,' said the wizard. 'Indeed, the War of the Roses is over. And…?'

Branok hesitated then ventured,

'The war for the throne of England is over?' asked Branok.

'Quite right, boy,' said Merlin, groaning as he clambered to his feet. 'I have brought peace to the land.'

'To England,' said Branok. Merlin froze then turned to regard his young pupil, a mere boy. Branok twirled blades of grass around his fingers and pulled at them until they snapped. The wizard frowned.

'What?' said the wizard, quietly and cautiously, sensing something, he knew not what, from the child.

Branok raised his eyes to look up at his mentor.

'The land is not yet united. King Henry rules over England and Wales, but still a lion dwells in the north untamed,' said Branok, and Merlin, seeing that the child was close to being in a trance, felt a cold shiver run up his spine. He stooped down and took the boy by the shoulders.

'Branok,' he said, shaking him slightly.

The boy started, drawing in a breath, and grasped Merlin's wrist.

'Tell me about Arthur again,' he said. 'Tell me of the king who slumbers.'

Merlin frowned and pulled Branok to his feet then brushed grass and dirt from his robes, buying himself time to think.

'How did you know what Arthur would become? How did you know which parents to give him?' Branok persisted, as though hungry.

Merlin turned to walk from the circle, and Branok trotted to keep up with the old wizard's pace.

He said nothing as foreboding arose in him, bile swilling in his stomach, for the boy had touched on a hidden thought. They reached a copse, and only when Merlin had reached its centre and found a fallen tree to sit upon did they speak again.

'Merlin!' Branok insisted with impetuousness that Merlin did not recognise in the boy. It was as though this new thought had kindled a fire within him.

'How could you know that King Uther would beget Arthur by the lady, Igraine?'

'You speak of it,' said Merlin slowly, 'as though I had advance knowledge of the outcome,' said Merlin, and as he finished speaking, he saw Branok's face fall in realisation that his mentor was not as all-knowing as he had supposed. Perhaps, thought Merlin, because the boy sees more than I do, his abilities outstripping my own.

'But you chose Uther and helped him trick Igraine into lying with him so that Arthur would be born, the king who would become legend and unite the land,' Branok insisted, but Merlin shook his head.

'No, boy, such a thing was beyond my ken,' Merlin admitted. 'Uther was the strongest and if the land was ever to unite, I believed he was the king to achieve it. Uther wanted Igraine, and it was against my better judgement that I used my arts to deceive her.'

Branok leaned forward, elbows on knees, and rubbed his eyes with the palms of his hands.

Merlin watched the boy musing on his words.

'Have I disappointed you, Branok?' said Merlin after a while.

The boy said nothing, just kept rubbing his eyes.

'Branok,' Merlin said again. 'What have you seen?'

At this the pupil took heed of his teacher and turned to him.

'A possibility,' said Branok.

'For?' asked Merlin.

'To secure peace for the land. The marriage yesterday united the royal houses of England, and yet Scotland remains apart. I have seen my purpose, Merlin. One land. One bloodline,' he said.

'I see,' said Merlin. 'You would have us unite the thrones of England and Scotland.'

Branok's eyes began to glaze over, and when he spoke it was as though the voice of an older man emerged from between his lips.

'The queen will give birth to two sons and two daughters,' said Branok.

He laughed and shook his head.

'The first son will be called Arthur,' he managed to say when the mirth had subsided, 'and yet he will not live to become king.'

Merlin gripped his staff so tightly that his knuckles turned white.

'The second son will grow to be King Henry VIII, and though he will have many children, three of whom will take the throne after him, his line will fail.'

Branok shuddered, and his eyes returned to normal.

'But there is a way, Merlin.'

'A way?' asked the wizard as his suspicion grew.

Branok said nothing.

'You have been meddling with the dark arts,' said Merlin. 'Such foresight is not granted to practitioners of the true magick.' The wizard got to his feet.

'There is no such thing as the dark arts, Merlin,' Branok implored, dropping to his feet and approaching his mentor, but Merlin shook his head.

'You are deluded, or have been beguiled,' he said. 'and I will teach you no more, Branok.'

The boy stopped, dropping his hands to his side.

'Merlin,' he said and the hurt in his voice pained the wizard.

'No, Branok,' the wizard shouted. 'This is witchcraft, plain and simple, of the blackest kind. Who has taught you?' He stormed forward, reaching to seize the boy, but as he did so, he felt as though his hand was pushing through gelatinous matter that irritated and burned. He drew back his hand.

Whatever it was, it was not coming from the boy, Merlin knew.

'The King's Coven,' Merlin whispered.

'Merlin, don't be angry. I'm sorry!' said Branok. 'Please, Merlin!'

But Merlin could hear them now, whispering and swarming around him, his cloak hitching and twitching as their ethereal fingers groped at him. His skin rippled with gooseflesh.

'Will you come away with me, if you are truly sorry?' Merlin asked without moving his lips, speaking directly to Branok's mind.

The boy hesitated, looking up at the sky as though listening.

'They showed me how to see, Merlin. I can heal the land and unite the thrones,' Branok insisted, and Merlin saw the first tear fall.

But the wizard shook his head.

'My arts derive from the land and the will of the people, Branok. Such sorcery as theirs is an unnatural, grasping thing that seeks to hew and change the fates with the aid of things summoned. You are in danger, my boy. You should know that, if I have taught you anything at all. We can pursue your ideas, but not with their assistance,' said Merlin.

Branok stood looking at the wizard, clutching his arms about him as though against a cold wind that did not blow.

Then he turned to run between the trees. Merlin watched him go.

Merlin took to his wandering once more, abandoning his apprentice. The realm was at peace as much as it ever could be, to the wizard's mind. In September of 1486, Merlin was lodging in the New Forest when he heard that the queen had given birth to a son, and that the young prince was named Arthur. The old wizard had set down his wine, feeling quite faint.

So, he thought, *the boy has true sight*, and he mourned for the prince whom he knew now was doomed to die before ever he inherited the throne, at least if Branok's vision was correct.

Branok plagued his dreams, and he suspected not as mere phantoms of his own mind. But Merlin did not acquiesce to the growing child's demands as the years went on, as Branok sought to persuade him that the thrones of England and Scotland could be united by the creation of his own contribution to legend, the breeding of his very own equivalent of Arthur.

And then, some three years after they had parted in the copse, word reached Merlin that another royal child had been born, who had been named Margaret.

It was at this time that Branok fell silent and quested for Merlin no more.

The wizard grew fearful.

Henry VII was a cautious, wily character, eager to secure his throne. He was a dour, frugal man, and wary of war with the Scots. Branok began by visiting the king in his dreams, cultivating the fear and positing possible solutions, and one chief among them.

Branok infiltrated the court itself and in time, manoeuvred himself behind the throne, so that he could, discreetly, whisper in the king's ear.

In January 1502, England and Scotland signed the Treaty of Perpetual Peace, and the marriage between Henry's daughter, Margaret Tudor, and James IV of Scotland was agreed, the result of Branok's whispering.

Branok could not yet rest, knowing full well he must support the couple over the years to come, for they would lose many children in infancy. In 1512 Margaret, Queen of Scots, gave birth to James, who would later become James V, and father Mary, Queen of Scots, who would give birth to King James VI of Scotland.

That James, when Queen Elizabeth I, the last Tudor monarch, died without an heir, would become King James VI of Scotland and James I of England, uniting Britain with one Royal bloodline.

Branok, his goal achieved, sought out the infant king and began a lifetime of service to both him and his descendants.

Chapter Five

October 2019

Arthur waited in the hall for Tristan to return, and only once he had a hot mug in his hand did he unlock the door to the drawing-room, wood-panelled, with windowless walls and an imposing fireplace. Arthur set his mug down on a table beside his favourite leather wingback chair then proceeded to build a fire in the grate. Once the flames had taken hold, he straightened up and stood a while, running his eyes along the lines of the great sword, mounted with its blade vertical, a few inches above the fireplace.

He lost track of time, and his reverie was only broken by the old man's voice behind him.

'How long has it been, boy?' he said.

Merlin stood in the doorway, a comical figure swathed in a white dressing gown and slippers.

'How long has what been?' asked Arthur.

'Since you took it up. Since you wielded it,' said Merlin.

'In battle?' Arthur ushered Merlin towards the other chair by the fire, and the old man made his way to sit.

'Coffee? Wine? Water?' asked Arthur, but Merlin shook

his head as he settled back into the chair.

Arthur lifted his mug to his lips.

'The last time I wielded Excalibur,' he said, as though to himself, staring into the flames. He cast his mind back over the years then nodded.

'Naseby. Summer of 1645,' he concluded.

'June 14th,' said Merlin, shaking his head. 'Near enough four hundred years.'

'A long time,' said Arthur.

'A long time to be idle,' said Merlin.

'Not idle, Merlin,' said Arthur, restraining his temper as best he could, yet not enough it seemed. Merlin raised an eyebrow in amusement, casting a sidelong look from his chair.

'Excalibur is of a bygone age,' said Arthur. 'Like us.'

'Speak for yourself, boy. I'm yet to hit my prime,' Merlin snapped. Arthur ignored him.

'A great sword was no use in the age of sabres and muskets, and is of even less with every passing year,' Arthur said.

'No use?' Merlin spat. 'The sword of legend, bound to the land? No use?'

Now it was Arthur's turn to raise his voice.

'Must you be so contrary? You know full well what I mean. A great sword is heavy to wield and its length can be a disadvantage. Excalibur may well cleave a man in half, but that's no use if you've been stabbed or shot full of holes between blows. Its time has passed.'

Merlin returned his gaze to the fire.

'We shall see in time,' was his knowing reply, distorted by a long yawn.

'Will we? Do you expect Queen Elizabeth to ride out against Al Qaida holding Excalibur high? Perhaps when the newspapers demand that Charles abdicate in favour of William, they can each attempt to draw the sword from the stone?' Arthur barked. Merlin's only reply was inaudible, grumbled under his breath.

The two men warmed themselves by the fire amid a brooding silence, each on their own side of a wall that could never be quite dismantled. Arthur knew that Merlin had never understood.

'Why have you come, Merlin?' asked Arthur eventually.

'They are calling for a referendum to abolish the monarchy,' said Merlin.

'I've seen as much in the newspapers,' said Arthur, sipping his Jamaican blend coffee. The taste was far superior to that at the café. This glorious brew from a noble bean of the new world never failed to transport Arthur over the sea and to those lands discovered in his absence. Every breath of its aroma called for him to take to the sea, or the air he supposed, and seek for those new places.

But no.

Here he was, as he had ever been, with the odd exception, in England.

'Did you also see,' pressed Merlin, 'that the ravens have left the Tower?'

This was news, and Arthur's eyes widened. He set down his mug and all thought of adventure.

'When?'

'Thursday,' said Merlin. 'No one knows how.'

Arthur jumped up and paced back and forth before the fireplace.

'This is ill news. Do you believe…?' he said, but Merlin cut him off.

'That Branok is awake. Aye. For certain.'

'And all of them have left? You're sure?' said Arthur.

'All six.'

'But even during the Blitz, one remained,' said Arthur, incredulous.

Merlin nodded. 'Grip. Ridiculous name for a bird.'

'All six,' Arthur repeated it to himself.

'All six,' said Merlin. 'Upped and left.'

'Or summoned,' said Arthur, his face grim. 'What do you suppose they are up to?'

'Who can tell?' said Merlin. 'But I believe with the talk of doing away with the monarchy, Branok may be moving against the people once more. I can but guess.'

Arthur leaned against the fireplace, looking up at Excalibur.

'Would you hear my counsel, boy?' said Merlin. 'Or will you snap at an old man for speaking his mind?'

Arthur turned and saw the old wizard's face broken by a lopsided smile.

'I'll hear you, you meddlesome imp,' Arthur sighed, 'but don't think I'm oblivious to the pleasure you're taking in this.'

'If the ravens are gone, Branok is surely awake and has

deployed his familiars. You must send out your knights against them, Arthur, lest they do us all great harm. And Branok must be put down, forever this time,' Merlin intoned, all humour gone from his voice.

Arthur locked eyes with the old man and searched for the truth of the matter. Eventually, he let out a breath and nodded.

'I'll send word for everyone to return in the morning,' he said, returning to his chair. He drank from his coffee once more.

'What do you suppose he's doing?' said Arthur.

'Branok will do whatever it takes to maintain the royal line, Arthur, and the monarchy has never been weaker. The people are turning their back on them. It's neither here nor there to me, understand. These daughters and sons of Norman invaders have no more right to sit on the throne than did the Saxons when first you rode to war.' The old man shifted in his seat, leaning forward towards Arthur. 'But I'll concede, I've taught you well, boy. You've some wisdom in you. What is England? The land, the Crown or the people? The land can look after itself well enough, it will endure. The Crown? The throne has been taken by whoever liked the look of it and was strong enough to take it for centuries, and the people aren't those you ruled over, Arthur, the people – Saxons, Britons, Normans, immigrants from all over the world. England is the land and the people, whoever may dwell upon it. Branok will never recognise that. All that matters to him is the blood. Stuart, by preference, but Windsor will do in the interim.

He'll do whatever it takes to ensure the people don't get what they want, even if it means killing every last one of them.'

'We'll stop him,' said Arthur.

'You haven't yet,' said Merlin. 'How many have died because of him?'

'This time we'll stop him,' said Arthur.

The phone rang during dinner, and Tristan went to answer it. He was gone for only a short time.

'Everyone can be back by morning except Bedivere.' said Tristan. 'And, of course, Agravain is still at Her Majesty's pleasure for the foreseeable future.'

'Good news,' said Arthur. 'Everyone is to meet in here at 9am sharp for briefing.' He smiled.

'I sound like a captain in a 1950s war film,' he laughed.

'To be fair, sir, you've a good excuse,' said Kay, also laughing as he pushed back his plate.

'Speaking of films, I believe I'll watch one then have an early night,' said Gareth.

'Count me in,' said Percival.

'Me too,' said Tristan. 'How about you, sir?'

Arthur shot a wicked smile at Merlin.

'Care to join us?' he said.

The old man frowned.

'Not if this is going to be a jest at my expense, no,' he said. 'I wearied of such japes in the 6th century. None of you ever grow up.'

Suppressing grins, Arthur and the others led Merlin into the small cinema located at the rear of the house.

Merlin sat through Excalibur, albeit sulking and muttering throughout, but left during the first animation in Monty Python and the Holy Grail.

‘Children,’ he railed as he disappeared, shutting the door behind him.

They waited as long as they could before the room filled with laughter.

‘What’s got his goat?’ asked Bors, tears rolling down his cheeks.

‘He’s just annoyed he’s not in it,’ said Tristan.

‘He had a stupid metal cap and talked funny in the first one, and he sat through that,’ exclaimed Kay.

‘You have bro-ken, what could not be bro-ken,’ intoned Arthur, in a passable impression of Nicol Williamson in the John Boorman epic.

‘Seriously though, where do they get those ideas from?’ said Kay.

Arthur shook his head.

‘It’s beyond me,’ he said.

‘Spill the beans, sir. Who’s this Guinevere then?’ said Tristan, elbowing Arthur in the arm.

‘I’m more interested in who this Lancelot represents…’ Arthur pointed at Tristan, Bors and Percival in turn, a stern look upon his face.

‘Sir, I’d never…’ said Percival.

'He's poking fun, you idiot,' said Tristan. 'Catch up.'

'Every time,' Kay rolled his eyes as Percival's cheeks reddened.

The following morning Arthur entered the dining room shortly before nine to find all of his knights seated at the round oak table, each groomed to within an inch of their lives and wearing their best suits. Merlin paced the edge of the room with his hands clasped behind his back, no longer looking homeless. He wore a tweed three-piece suit, and his white hair was pulled back into a ponytail.

Arthur stood behind his chair and told them all that he knew.

'And so,' he concluded, 'we'll need to call on all our contacts, pool our resources and begin an investigation. We must find Branok, find the ravens and stop them, but we must also identify their targets and protect them if we can.'

He sat down with his men.

'I'll need six volunteers to seek out Branok's familiars,' said Arthur, producing a notepad and pen from his inside pocket. He opened the book and made ready with the pen then looked up at them all.

They all put themselves forward, even if their words were lost in the commotion. Arthur tapped the nib on the paper and then scrawled across first one page then the next.

'Right, I'll have Kay, Tristan, Gawain, Dagonet, Lucan and Ector on the ground. The rest of you will start by working the phones, reading the papers and talking to our friends in Westminster,' said Arthur.

He turned to Merlin.

'Would you like to add anything?'

The old wizard lowered his brow as he crossed the room to stand beside and just behind Arthur's chair. He looked up and fixed each of them with a stare one at a time.

'I will aid you in this task, but on one condition,' he said, his voice grave.

'State it,' said Kay.

Tristan was already beginning to grin.

'I will not, under any circumstances, sit through any film in which Richard Gere plays a knight of Arthur's court,' he said and then, as they began to laugh, he pointed straight at Percival.

'I saw the cover of the DVD, do you think me a fool?'

And as Percival leapt to his own defence, Arthur sat back in his chair, watching the scene play out, all too conscious that the time for merriment would soon be at an end.

Chapter Six

Edinburgh – 1597

King James sits upon the throne of Scotland.
Queen Elizabeth I yet reigns in England.

The corridors of Holyrood Palace were lined with armed men and yet they made no move against Branok as he stalked the halls towards King James's chambers. Instead, they nodded in deference to the man they *thought* they recognised as a result of his enchantments.

He entered the king's bedchamber without knocking and secured it behind him.

Branok moved to the side of James's bed and shook the sleeping man's foot. The king started awake and sat up in bed, pushing himself back against the headboard and blinking.

'Is this how you repay me? You owe me for your very existence, boy!' hissed Branok.

King James VI of Scotland eyed the warlock and his gaze shifted to the door as though contemplating calling for help, but Branok held a pamphlet aloft and hurled it toward the king. The pamphlet fell short and landed facing upwards on the bedclothes, its title, 'Daemonologie', clear for James to see.

As he did so, James nodded and composed himself.

'It's been many years, Branok,' he said. 'and much has changed in that time.'

'It would seem so!' Branok roared, and yet the guards outside did not stir. James sat up a little straighter.

'James, son of Mary, daughter of James, daughter of Margaret, daughter of Henry,' Branok recited, flicking out a finger as he counted each of the king's ancestors.

'Each of them knew their place, knew their role. Knew how they came to power.'

Branok scuttled around the bed and stood over the king, his chest heaving and eyes bloodshot.

'And you have turned against us all! The blood in your veins is precious, and in time you will unite Great Britain and Ireland. And yet it is my doing! By my arts! The very arts you so utterly condemn in that piece of heresy!' With this final word, Branok slammed his hand down upon the pamphlet and, in so doing, the leg of the king, who remained placid as the warlock raged.

'I sat idly by as you attended witch trials that condemned innocents to death, thinking that it was but a phase, perhaps the influence of your new bride. But years pass and now this? Satanism, necromancy, sorcery and witchcraft, all thrown together and condemned. This is nothing short of a call to arms against what is left of my kind! And why? What did I do, oh king, to offend thee so?' said Branok, and finally his tirade was at an end. He sat down upon the edge of the bed and waited for an answer, for repentance and for succour.

'You are in a pact with the Devil, sir,' said King James, his voice calm, 'and your arts are an abomination against the Lord our God. As his representative on this Earth, it is my duty and my pleasure to root out your kind and see them sent back to hell, sir. If I have been fortunate enough to land in this position, it is through God's work not yours, and you blaspheme by suggesting otherwise. I have broken your coven, Branok, as I will break your hold on my family. It is by my affection alone that you survive, but you will not attend court again. Now leave Scotland, and remember that if I hear of you again, the full might of the law will be used against you.'

Branok, hands shaking, stood, and he looked down upon James, the king that he had created, the boy who was to be his, as Arthur belonged to Merlin. He backed away a step.

'You will not see me again, boy, and you may go on despising me,' he said at last, licking his dry lips. 'but I will be watching over you nonetheless. The blood in your veins is sacred indeed, but not because there is one on high who deems it so. You will have a son, Charles, and perhaps he will know me better than does his father.'

Branok turned and stalked from the room then on through the castle, his eyes brimming with tears. He fled out into the night and found his horse then rode hard southward towards England as though the drumming of hooves might drown out the recriminations running through his mind.

The years wore on, and Branok entered the employ of Sir Robert Carey, taking up residence in a small cottage on the family estate. He practised his arts and kept abreast of the news of the day in the dwindling years of the reign of Elizabeth I of England and Ireland. James VI's queen gave him first a son, Henry, and yet Branok's divinations told him the boy would not live. A fear grew in him that James's malevolence against the powers of his making had soured his seed, but, to his great relief, the queen gave birth to another son, Charles, in 1600. As the infant drew his first breath, Branok stirred in his bed and knew that a future king had been born - Charles I of Great Britain.

In March 1603, Branok received word that Queen Elizabeth had died, and at that moment, he knew that his plans had come to fruition and his predictions come to pass. Sure enough, James VI of Scotland was declared King of England and Ireland, and before long, the king came south, as Branok had known he would.

London – 4th of November 1605
The Loneliest Moment

In the undercroft below the House of Lords, a single figure waited silently in the gloom beside thirty-six barrels of gunpowder, disguised with firewood. In a cloak and hat, Guy Fawkes waited.

The months of planning, of brotherhood, of rallying cries and the secret confidence of men working together were over. Suddenly, and finally, it all came down to him, Fawkes thought, one man sitting beside not only enough ordnance to send King James VI & I to hell with all his lords, but a pile of evidence so large that should it fall on him, he would never lever it off.

The waiting was interminable, listening to the rats scurrying around his feet and water dripping from the vaulted ceilings. Minutes turned to hours while Fawkes waited, all the time battling with himself, fighting the urge to abandon this plan and escape while he still could. And yet in the light of day how would he justify his actions to his co-conspirators? He could not stand the shame.

Time passed. Fawkes set a trail of gunpowder from the barrels in the direction of his way of escape. He stood and began to leave then stopped short and cursed aloud. Fawkes returned to his seat, cold sweat beading his forehead. He pinched the bridge of his nose and said a silent prayer.

Shortly after midnight, Fawkes stepped out of the cellar to stretch his legs and there saw a band of men searching beneath the Houses of Parliament. Fawkes reached out with his left hand and seized the man closest to him and it looked as though the man would draw his knife, but instead he cried out, hurling Fawkes onto his face. The party set about searching him, and Fawkes knew that all was lost.

'Sir,' said Branok and the leader of the men

turned to look at him. Branok held out a slow match that Fawkes had discarded before being taken, the instrument with which he was to have set the gunpowder alight. Branok handed it over and moved into the cellar. Sure enough, the intelligence his familiar had gathered was correct. Barrels of gunpowder.

Fawkes was dragged away, and once the body of men was clear of the tunnels, Branok took the earliest opportunity to break away from the group, and wandered to a place beside the river from where he could look upon the Houses of Parliament, thinking of disaster averted and the now estranged king whose life he had saved.

Branok sensed his familiar was near. He looked down and saw a brown rat, sitting on its hindquarters looking up at him.

Branok stooped and lifted the creature. It crawled up his arm and came to rest upon his shoulder. Branok looked around to ensure he was alone and then spoke softly to it.

'You have done well, and will be rightly rewarded, my child,' he said. 'but first we must seek out the conspirators. Come away with me to some quiet place, and you must tell me all that you have learnt.'

Slipping his familiar into his pocket, Branok walked towards his lodgings, casting his eyes up towards Parliament with a bitter feeling growing in his heart.

Branok returned to Sir Robert Carey's estate after news of the foiled plot had been announced to the wider world.

He visited Carey's wife, Elizabeth, and her young charge just as soon as he had relinquished his outer clothing.

Charles, Duke of York, but four years old, skirted the room using furniture for support, boots of Spanish leather supporting his weak ankles. Branok went to the boy and knelt beside him.

'Charles,' he whispered when first they had a moment alone together.

The boy who would be king looked into Branok's eyes.

'I have brought you a present,' Branok said, and the prince's eyes lit up as the warlock handed over a box secured with a ribbon.

Branok seated himself in a comfortable chair by an open fire and revelled in the boy's pleasure as he revealed his treat.

Chapter Seven

The English Civil War: 1642
War between the forces of
Parliament and Charles I.

Merlin sat upon a log, running his eyes over a patch of deadly nightshade while he waited, contemplating its uses and its perils. A stag wandered into the glade and it froze, staring straight at Merlin, but he gave it a little nod and the animal relaxed and went about its business without further concern.

Merlin leaned on his staff and closed his eyes, drifting off for a time. He woke suddenly and saw the stag bolting across the glade. It leapt into the air and disappeared between the trees just as a flock of birds took to the skies.

'Subtle as ever,' Merlin muttered and straightened up, stretching so that his back cracked. He stood and, closing his eyes again momentarily, reaching out, he turned to face the direction from which he knew the newcomer would emerge.

Sure enough, Branok stepped into the glade and looked around, as though expecting some kind of ambush.

The two practitioners watched each other carefully as Branok drew near. Then, as former pupil or as someone who just wanted something from him, Merlin could not yet decide which, he bowed low in a gesture of respect.

Merlin nodded to the other man, leaning on his staff, an eyebrow raised, waiting for the reason for this reacquaintance to become apparent, though he had suspicions.

'You're looking well,' said Branok, shooting Merlin a nervous smile.

'Shall we address the business at hand,' said Merlin, frowning. 'I've better things to do than pretend we like one another, child.'

Anger flashed across Branok's face though Merlin's smile was genuine.

'Go ahead,' said Merlin. 'I'll hear you out.' The wizard sat back down on his log.

Branok came to stand before him and for a moment, their dynamic mimicked that of years before they had drifted apart.

'Bring him back,' said Branok. 'The time has come, Merlin.'

'Oh, indeed?'

'I believe so,' said Branok. 'Do you not see what is going on in this country? King Charles has fled London and set up his court in Oxford. There is war between Parliament and the throne.'

'I am well aware, thank you,' Merlin snapped. 'What do you take me for?'

Branok did not answer.

'The people are divided. Brothers fight brothers. Fathers fight sons. Men die for vagaries of religious interpretation. Charles has made some unfortunate decisions,' said Branok, 'but…'

Merlin's laugh interrupted him.

'King Charles has signed his own death warrant, mark my words, boy,' said Merlin.

Branok stalked towards him, but restrained his temper.

'That is not a foregone conclusion. Bring Arthur back. I've read the legends. And you taught me how he could rally and inspire the people. He could quell this rebellion and return to slumber,' said Branok.

Merlin brooded on Branok's words, and could not deny that something stirred within him at the thought of seeing Arthur again.

He sighed and tapped the far end of the log with his staff. Branok took the hint and came to sit beside him.

'Are you still practising the forbidden arts?' asked Merlin.

'Hardly forbidden. You simply disapprove, and in truth, Merlin, you are not above using them yourself!'

'Only in great need, and out of desperate love, and I will only do so once more,' said Merlin, conceding the point, but feeling the need to qualify it.

'Nevertheless,' said Branok.

Merlin studied the deadly nightshade and clicked his tongue against his teeth.

'The world is a very different place. A millennium has passed since Arthur walked in the world. It was a time when one man could lead an army to change the country; a time when a strong leader might make a difference. In this era of courts and parliaments, of intrigue and rebellion, I am not sure what role Arthur would play.'

Merlin smiled wistfully to himself.

'I acted in haste at Camlann and have burdened us all with a great weight of expectation. He must come again, and perhaps it should be now, before the world grows any more alien, lest he cannot cope at all.'

He looked across at Branok.

'I can offer you no assurance that he will assist the House of Stuart, or even if he can assist,' said Merlin. 'Arthur is no mere puppet to be controlled through sorcery.'

'Influenced, maybe,' he said under his breath, to himself.

'If he will not assist the House of Stuart, I am sure he will not thwart us, he who was himself a king!' said Branok.

'Do you also remember, in your excitement, of how he came to fall through his own actions, by Mordred's hand?' asked Merlin. 'Do not be hasty-minded, Branok.'

Branok said nothing, thinking only of Arthur's ability as a war leader, of how he could take the mastery of Charles's armies and lead them to victory.

Merlin sighed and stood.

'Very well,' he said. 'Let the prophecy work its power. Let us draw this matter of wizards and kings to a close, for good or ill. Follow.'

And together teacher and student made their way back to the place where they had last seen one another, over a century before.

They reached Stonehenge in the early hours of the morning, when the way was lit only by the light of the moon and stars. Both men sensed a tension in the air as they approached the great standing stones in their looming circle.

Merlin closed his eyes, reaching out to

discern if there were any nearby, but, satisfied that there was no one, he opened them again and stood beside a stone. Branok drew in beside him, wringing his hands.

Merlin caught the fidgeting out of the corner of his eye. He turned on Branok, taking him by the shoulder and spoke stern words to him.

'You are going to be disappointed, boy. Arthur is just a man, for the most part. Do not think we are summoning Thor or Mars. Put that notion out of your mind,' said Merlin. Branok frowned and looked back to the circle.

Merlin reached out with his staff, and laying his other hand upon the stone beside him, he began to speak in that same ancient tongue he had used at Camlann, finishing the verse he had begun a millennium before.

Nothing happened.

Merlin leaned on his staff from the exertion, nearly in a swoon, and Branok steadied him.

'What now?' said Branok, and Merlin scoffed.

'I forgot you would be unable to see,' he remarked and waved his hand over Branok's eyes. 'There are two powers at work here; one to seal the entrance and another to disguise it.'

When the warlock looked back across the circle, he saw what looked like a single open grave in the very centre. Merlin led him towards it and, standing at one end, began to descend a steep set of stairs downwards. They ended abruptly and a corridor sloped even further down. There was no light at all to see by and yet Merlin walked on as confidently as if he was strolling in a field under the noon sun. Branok felt his way along the wall, trying to keep up, stumbling here and there. The passage began to spiral downwards.

Finally a faint light became visible up ahead, and Merlin strode towards it at a renewed pace.

He stepped into a cavernous hall with earth walls, around which stood crude statues of men who held ancient broadswords at their chests, tips pointed towards the ground. In the centre of the room stood an immense round table, which looked to be made of English oak.

Atop it lay Arthur and his knights, laid out on their backs a little distance apart with their feet at the table's centre. They wore simple clothing, all save Arthur who also wore a silver circlet upon his brow and whose hands were clasping the hilt of Excalibur in the same manner as the statues around the room.

Branok stood beside Merlin and looked around in awe.

'I knew, but I didn't believe, I can see that now,' said Branok in a hushed tone.

'Welcome to an old man's folly,' said Merlin and then, louder, he spoke a single word in an ancient tongue. And Branok listened well.

The men on the table let out a collective gasp, causing Branok to jump. Arthur and his knights started where they lay, breathing fast. As they came to their senses, they sat up, looking around at one another.

Kay caught sight of Merlin.

'How long has it been?' he said.

'A long time,' said Merlin, and Branok noticed tears were streaming down the wizard's cheeks. He advanced upon the table and clasped the hands of the knights as he passed them by as he made his way round to Arthur.

The former king sat with his knees up to his chest, rubbing his eyes with his fingertips. He shuddered as Merlin and Branok, standing a little behind Merlin, stopped before him.

'I don't understand,' said Arthur. 'I slipped into dark water. I don't know this place.'

'It is well, for if you were aware of the passage of time here, I fear you would be quite mad,' said Merlin. He stepped forward and took Arthur's hand.

'It has been a long, long time, my boy,' he said and drew Arthur towards him. The younger man, puzzled, took the wizard to him in an embrace, his white hair pressed against Arthur's chest.

'Merlin?'

'Do not ask me too many questions, boy. I haven't the heart to answer them. You passed on, but you are back now. For now, that is all that matters,' said Merlin, drawing back and smiling.

'There is much work to be done,' said Branok. 'I need your sword.'

Arthur looked down at Excalibur.

'He means in the abstract sense, boy,' tutted Merlin. 'Well, mostly. I see a millennium at rest has done nothing to consolidate your meagre wits.'

A ripple of quiet laughter around the table, and the knights gathered to Arthur, obviously overcome with relief at seeing him intact and breathing once more.

When he had greeted them all, embraced them all, he turned his attention to Branok.

'I don't remember you,' he said.

'I am Branok. I asked Merlin to bring you back now because England is in great need of the legendary King Arthur.'

'Legendary?' said Arthur.

'Hmm,' said Merlin.

Arthur's stomach growled, and he looked around for water.

'There will be time for business later, Branok. For now, let's get you all above ground, fed and watered. We must find you attire and lodgings. Then we will talk,' said Merlin.

'There *is* much to discuss,' said Branok.

Arthur looked into the man's eyes, and he felt his spirits dampen.

Merlin waved a hand towards the passage to the surface.

'Lay on, Macduff,' he said.

'What?' asked Arthur.

Merlin sighed.

'There is much I will need to teach you.'

Chapter Eight

The English Civil War:
The Battle of Marston Moor – 1644

Branok awoke with a start, cold sweat soaking his hair. The battle had gone ill, the Royalist forces were defeated. And Boye? Prince Rupert had tied him up at camp before the battle, but Branok knew now that his familiar, now in the shape of a dog, was in danger itself. It had broken free. It had followed Rupert into the battle and now...

Branok watched Prince Rupert of the Rhine and his cavalry retreat through his familiar's eyes, his fingernails cutting into the flesh of his palms until blood coursed between his fingers and dripped to the summer grass, his body shaking.

At least Rupert has survived, thought Branok. *At least all is not lost.*

He closed his eyes and reached out with his mind to his familiar, but Boye could not hear him, caught as he was in a frenzy of pain and terror.

Branok concentrated, and his knees buckled so that he sunk down upon them before collapsing on his side. He heard the thumping cannon and the screams with the dog's ears now, though they were miles distant. He smelt the burnt gunpowder as the smoke drifted across the field.

Boye was surrounded, Branok saw, the white curls of his fur matted with blood from the multitude of wounds he had suffered whilst trying in vain to reach his master.

And for what? Prince Rupert did not need our protection today, it seems.

The Parliamentarian soldiers pricked Boye, slashed at him with their swords, laughing and howling with a ferocity that could only been driven by fear. They knew the white hunting poodle for what it was; he had after all accompanied Prince Rupert constantly through every battle of the conflict. They had heard the rumours that if a musket ball was about to hit the general, Boye could snatch it from the air with his mouth, that he could hunt out treasures, and they had heard of his fiendish capabilities, wrongly believing him to be Rupert's familiar, some spirit or even the devil himself in animal form, summoned by the prince's witchcraft. They had heard how Boye could not be killed. Branok saw the fear in their eyes, their wild faces and their desperate attacks. They did not seem to see the dog whimpering and snarling, weakening and failing, how he had ceased lunging and biting.

'Kill it,' screamed one man as he levelled his musket and pulled the trigger.

And then, like a candle extinguished by a winter gust, Boye was gone, and Branok was lying in far-off mud, weeping and alone on the hillside.

He lay there for what seemed like hours, disconnected and abandoned, until he heard the sound of hooves approaching up the slope from the battlefield.

'Is he dead?' said a voice.

'Use your eyes, Percival,' said another, and many others shared the speaker's chuckle.

'Hush,' said another, more familiar voice.

Branok, bereft as he was, finally paid attention to the present and pushed aside his grief as he heard someone drop from their saddle into the mud just yards from where he lay.

Men on horseback had formed a line along the ridge, men in long black boots and soldiers' coats with Roundhead lobster helms on their heads and cavalry sabres at their sides.

One man only had dismounted, clad in similar fashion, but with a red officer's sash around his waist and a broad-brimmed hat instead of a helm. He was girt with an ancient broadsword, which hung from his belt in a battered leather scabbard, quite out of keeping with his immaculate uniform.

His blue eyes were keen and a brown beard flecked with grey disguised his lower face.

'Are you injured, Branok?' said Arthur, standing before the fallen man and offering his hand.

Branok leapt to his feet.

'You fought for Parliament?' he shouted, once more balling his fists. 'You of all people?'

In seconds, four more of the men had dismounted and were advancing on him, swords drawn, but Arthur checked their progress with a wave of his hand.

'You know me better than that, Branok,' said Arthur. 'but Parliament did win the field this day, and we have no desire to be caught as Royalists, though I am full aware of the irony. We must needs escape the field to advance our cause elsewhere,' he concluded.

Arthur reached out and grasped Branok's wrist then hauled him to his feet.

'What renders you as naught but a bundle of sobbing rags in the dirt?' Arthur asked.

Branok took control of his breathing and

wiped away tears with his forearm. He almost rebuked Arthur for his stark words, but saw only pity in the man's face.

'Boye,' he said, quiet so only Arthur could hear.

Arthur frowned.

'I cannot offer you sympathies for your loss, Branok. That business is beyond my understanding and, in truth, I cannot condone it. Perhaps Merlin would better understand your motives and your grief, but alas, he is not amongst us,' said Arthur.

Branok laughed, a cruel and humourless sound.

'So says Arthur, whose legacy utterly depends on the antics of a wizard in ages past!'

'Whatever Merlin may be, he is no witch,' said Arthur. The words fell with weight.

Branok shrugged, wanting nothing more than to be free of this man and this place, to find comfort elsewhere.

'Where now then?' said Arthur. 'We would be willing to escort you to safety.'

'I go wherever Prince Rupert goes,' said Branok. 'If you will not take up arms, then he may be King Charles's only hope of victory.'

'So be it. Our paths lie in different directions,' said Arthur.

'Unless you can be persuaded,' said Branok.

'I am resolute,' said Arthur.

'You could unite the people, Arthur. End this war,' Branok pleaded, admonishing himself silently as he did so. Would he truly allow himself to be drawn into this once more.

At this Galahad spurred his horse on and looked down at Branok, diminutive and sullen in his mud-covered cloak.

'Did you look out upon the field today?' he asked.

Branok looked up to meet his gaze, making no answer.

'I saw, what,' Galahad looked at Arthur for assistance, 'Thirty, maybe forty thousand English troops making war against one another today?' Arthur made no response and Galahad returned his attention to Branok.

'I did not see a people that is prepared to be united. Today the people won a battle against their king, who believes he rules over them by divine right, despite their discontent. And you would ask Arthur to add to this anarchy?'

'They would pay heed to Arthur!' Branok shouted, almost shrieked.

'They would not,' said Arthur. 'The world has moved on. We were summoned in vain, Branok. England is not ready, and may never be.'

'What then? You will turn coat to blend in with the victors at the close of every battle? Watch your own backs and raise your banner if and when it suits you?' spat Branok.

Tristan stormed forward and seized Branok by his coat.

'You speak boldly, witch, and against one you claim to support. Have a care,' said Tristan. Branok smiled, seeing the knight attempting to master his temper.

'Arthur has made his position quite clear, lapdog, but my duty is to Charles and his line. Where does your duty lie, Arthur?' Branok pulled back against Tristan's tightening grip as he turned, feeling the knight's breath breaking against his cheek.

'My duty is to England,' said Arthur. 'And I can do only what I can. Release him, Tristan, we must be away. There is nothing we can do here.'

Branok backed away.

'Aye, ride away, Arthur. Ride fast and do not look back. I will not forget you abandoned Charles in his time of need,' Branok promised. He stood silently as Arthur's men returned to their saddles and rode off down the hillside once more.

Merlin's boy, he thought. *A dream and nothing more.*

Branok did not follow Prince Rupert immediately. The word in the surrounding villages was that he had retreated to York with the remaining Royalist forces. Instead, Branok spent several days sleeping under hedgerows and in abandoned buildings while he waited for the aftermath of the battle to settle into nothing. On the third night after the battle, he returned to the desolate moors and walked out upon the scarlet grass, the souls of the thousands of newly dead crowding round him, breathing on the back of his neck and clawing at him in vain. He paid them no heed, though for the most part, they had fought for his king and for that, he knew, he owed them courtesy. But his mind was taken up with other matters for the present.

This was the first decisive loss for Prince Rupert and deep in his guts, Branok feared it heralded many more, that this war would end as had no other. That the throne would sit empty and another would rule. He knew it, he foresaw it.

There, making use of the items within his satchel, Branok drew his circle. He placed his tokens, and he began the ritual. The spirits of the dead rushed him and trampled his will. He fought back, pushing his way through them and clawing for air, though his body remained perfectly still within the circle. He spoke with them, vetted them and selected from among them. And then his will gave out, and Branok collapsed within the circle, knowing nothing more.

He awoke at dawn to the sound of ravens cawing as though within his own head. He opened his eyes, seeing only dew-covered grass. He shivered and ached, but moved slowly until he was sitting up.

Six ravens, one standing at each point of the pentagram within the circle and one at the very centre. Branok laughed and nodded to each in turn. The ravens lowered their heads one by one then called out in unison.

Branok closed his eyes and reached out for them, still shivering.

'Branok,' a voice rasped.

He opened his eyes. The ravens were gone and in their place were six naked people, three men and three women. They each smiled and then let out a caw. The sound resonated behind Branok's eyes, and his vision blurred. For a moment, he saw them as ravens once more. Ravens taking flight. Flying south.

Then Branok lost consciousness once more.

He awoke a short time later and was alone. He reassembled his satchel and set out back to his lodgings in Long Marston to prepare for his journey to York.

Chapter Nine

October 2019

Bare branches swayed in the chill wind, and leaves swirled around Branok as he strolled along the Serpentine in Hyde Park, hands in the pockets of his greatcoat, collar turned up.

He frowned as the sound of a wailing siren became audible even above the rushing sound of traffic and shook his head as he turned down towards Hyde Park Corner, walking along tarmac paths bordered by neatly kept grass. He crossed over Knightsbridge and stopped for a few minutes to take in the war memorial then snorted with contempt and turned his back. Branok passed through Wellington Arch before walking on along Constitution Hill with the wall to Buckingham Palace gardens to his right.

He reached out and allowed the soft pads of his fingertips to trail against the rough stone as he walked, savouring his closeness to the occupants of the palace beyond. Ahead of him, a figure bundled with coats, scarves and a hat, legs in a sleeping bag, sat up against the wall. A plastic cup weighed down with a few coins sat on the adjacent ground.

The figure did not move as Branok drew closer. The

warlock reached down and laid a hand on the figure's shoulder. She looked up at him, slowly, and her eyes, irises as black as her pupils, held an agelessness and nobility that belied her grubby skin and the reek that surrounded her. She peered up at him through greasy, tangled black hair.

Branok smiled, squeezing her shoulder, and she acknowledged him with the smallest of nods.

'The others?' asked Branok.

'We are watching, as we have ever done,' Daisy replied.

Branok crouched beside her, his coat puddling around him as he did so.

'My dear, you have done far more than that,' he said.

'Perhaps,' said Daisy, maintaining eye contact, a smile hiding just below the surface of her placid face. She lit a cigarette and offered one to Branok, who shook his head.

'Fetch your brothers and sisters, and bring them to the Banqueting House. We will assemble there,' said Branok. 'There, where it ended.'

Daisy nodded, and Branok stood then walked on along Constitution Hill. He looked back only once and saw that Daisy was gone. The plastic cup full of coins remained, sitting abandoned on the pavement. A raven's caw faded as the bird flew west towards Kensington.

Branok walked on, pausing for a short while to cast his eye over Buckingham Palace when he reached the front. He stood by the railings, accompanied only by tourists and the odd courting couple. He surveyed the many windows and noted the Coldstream Guards in their red tunics and towering bearskin hats. The palace was impressive, for certain, and Branok had no concerns for its security. How different it was to the Palace of Whitehall where the Stuart kings had ruled, now long burned to the ground, only the Banqueting House still standing.

He walked on down the Mall then cut along a path through St James's Park and Horse Guards Parade, through the arch in the grand buildings of Horse Guards themselves.

Branok stood on Whitehall, now nothing more than a road with as much traffic as any of those nearby. He looked up at the Banqueting House then crossed the road, darting between oncoming taxis to stand before the building. Near the corner, mounted on the wall above head height was a bronze bust, the sight of which forced Branok to choke back tears of rage and loss. He read the plaque below, which began:

King Charles I
1625 – 1649

Branok shivered as he looked up at the statue as though in expectation that the likeness of his friend and king would look down to meet his gaze.

Passers-by paid Branok no heed, for he was dressed as one of them, just a man looking up at yet another historic building. He clasped the railings while he waited, thinking back on the day when he had stood in this very place, how he had come to prevent the king's execution. How his best efforts had been foiled.

'My lord,' said Daisy, and Branok stepped back to greet

her, mastering his building emotions, but not so much that the dull ache in his chest disappeared.

His six familiars stood before him. The ravens of the Tower formed a tight semi-circle a few paces behind him.

Daisy with her black eyes and hair, studded leather jacket and boots. She wore a T-shirt with a band logo. Daisy appeared no more than nineteen, cigarette in hand, a fog of smoke about her.

Joseph, taller than the rest, black of beard, eyes of pure white though he was not blind, but he did carry a white cane nonetheless.

Faith, plaited red hair with jet beads tied within, a long brown coat hanging down by her booted feet. Shocking red eyes, and a guitar case in hand.

Martha, tinted glasses disguising golden eyes, wearing a pinstripe trouser suit and holding a briefcase.

Isaac, lithe and dressed in a green paramedic jumpsuit. His eyes were shocking blue and his hair was blonde.

Nathaniel, appearing no more than five. His irises were silver, and his fingers grasped Faith's coat.

Branok cleared his throat, resisting the urge to clasp his familiars to him.

'I go from a corruptible to an incorruptible Crown, where no disturbance can be,' he recited Charles I's words with ease, as they had haunted him for centuries.

'An incorruptible Crown,' he repeated as if to himself before stepping forward into their semi-circle.

They tilted their heads, out of sync with one another, turning, snapping their heads round, he supposed out of habit, to look at him from the corners of their eyes. He half expected them to caw when first they spoke.

'Better a corruptible Crown than no Crown at all,' said Nathaniel in his high, child's voice.

The rest nodded once, as one.

'The Crown may have been stripped of its political power, but it has endured and is more stable than it ever has been. The blood endures, and yet the people of this Great Britain would turn the monarch and her kin out into the street. I will not allow it, my children,' said Branok. He reached out and caressed Martha's jaw with the back of his fingers. 'Not again.'

'The people must be made to see their worth,' said Daisy.

Joseph snorted a laugh.

'The only time they see their worth is when one of them marries, one of them dies or when the country is under threat,' he said. 'They adore a spectacle.'

Branok moved to stand before Joseph, looking into his white eyes.

'Insightful as ever, Joseph,' he said, smiling, and the raven understood.

'They're all married now, at least the more prominent amongst them,' said Martha.

'Kill and threaten then,' said Nathaniel in his sing-song voice, playing at standing on one leg.

Branok frowned.

'This is no place to plot,' he said. 'Go now and make your way in the world as best you can. I will summon each of you in turn, and we will make our plans.'

Faith reached for Nathaniel's hand, and she led him away, appearing for all intents and purposes a young mother and son. Joseph bade Branok farewell and walked slowly towards the road, tapping and sweeping the pavement with his white cane.

Isaac, Martha and Daisy filtered into the crowds that walked the pavements. Immediately they were lost to Branok's eyes, but not his vision. He sensed them very well indeed.

He grasped the rails once more and stared up at the cold, immoveable statue, the likeness of Charles staring out across Whitehall, as if through the buildings in the direction of Buckingham Palace.

'I will do all I can, my friend,' Branok said aloud, heedless of those around him. A woman took a tight hold on her handbag and gave him a wide berth.

'I failed you all those years ago, but I have made up for it since,' Branok hissed. 'I returned your boy to power and restored the crown to his head. Your family wear it still. Perhaps when I see you again, my successes will merit your forgiveness.'

Charles's gaze remained fixed above the heads of his people.

As it should, I suppose, thought Branok. *As it should.*

A gust set him shivering, and his mind turned to more earthly concerns – a roof over his head and food in his belly. But where and how in this infernal place, this abomination of the London he had known?

Branok sought shelter.

Chapter Ten

Monday 29th of January 1649
Charles I is a prisoner of the Parliamentarians.
He has been found guilty of treason.

The raven settled on a window ledge of St. James's Palace and peered in through the glass, shaking out its wings and observing the scene within. Through the raven's eyes, Branok saw King Charles I embrace the sobbing Princess Elizabeth, just 11 years old, to his breast, fighting back his own tears as he did his best to calm her.

'Sweetheart, you will forget this,' said Charles, his voice soothing but trembling ever so slightly.

The raven, Isaac, watched as the king bade his two youngest children obey their older brother, Charles, soon to be the rightful king, and then the bird flew out across Hyde Park in search of Branok. He found the warlock crouching by one of the river Westbourne's many ponds. Isaac landed and, the change itself imperceptible, he appeared in the form of a high-born youth with fine clothes and a wispy beard.

'He is too well guarded,' concluded Branok before Isaac could give his report.

'Whether we kill one soldier or a thousand, I do not believe that we can prevent this, lord,' said Isaac.

'Perhaps not,' said Branok. 'but I will not allow it to go unopposed. Daisy has her task, and there is hope we may free him yet.'

4am - Tuesday 30th of January 1649

Shortly before dawn, Richard Brandon, the public executioner, held out his goblet so a serving girl could fill it with wine. Brandon thanked her and drank deep. He set down the goblet on the desk before him then returned to his diary.

He dipped the nib of a quill in an inkwell and continued writing. He wrote of the task before him the next morning, and of how when tasked with beheading the king, he had refused. He wrote of the threats directed at his family should he fail in his duty, but he never finished recording the thought. Richard Brandon's eyelids drooped and the strokes of his quill became ever more erratic until finally his head slumped forward so that his chin hit his chest. He dropped his quill, and his flailing arm knocked aside the goblet, spilling the fine red so that it streamed across the oak surface of the desk. It flowed over the edge of the table and stained the floor.

The door to his study opened, and the serving girl entered the room already carrying a cloth. She saw Brandon in his collapsed state and, without hesitation, moved to his side. She righted the goblet, and mopped up the wine and sedative with the cloth. Daisy, Branok's familiar, looked down upon the executioner, her eyes solid black. She read from his diary over his shoulder then plucked it from the desk and, after a moment of consideration, she threw the book into the fireplace where it kindled to flame. Quietly, she locked the room behind her and left the house to go out into the night.

But Daisy did not pass unnoticed. Merlin watched her go from the shadows and set out after her. He followed her as she turned left and right, seemingly at random through the streets. Merlin rounded a corner and could see the girl no more, but arrived in time to watch a raven take flight from the ground ahead of him and power skyward. Merlin watched her go.

10.00am – Tuesday 30th of January 1649

The following morning, Branok joined the assembling crowd before the Banqueting House at the Palace of Whitehall. The scaffold was complete and the block in place on the sand-strewn boards. Hundreds of people crammed in as close as they could to witness the unthinkable, to see the death of a king. Branok moved as near as the soldiers would allow, but they maintained the cordon at such a distance that it would be impossible to hear anything from the scaffold. He closed his eyes and concentrated, trying to shut out the many voices and the weight of sorrowful, excited expectation in the air. He reached out to his familiars, heart beating fast. The time had come.

Arthur, employed as a soldier, lifted the black cloak and draped it over Charles's shoulders, feeling as much a traitor as a man can, escorting a fellow king to a premature death.

'Thank you,' said Charles.

'Your Highness,' said Arthur, stepping back and bowing his head.

They set out from St James's Palace and walked through the park, the king, his attendant and a bishop surrounded on all sides by soldiers, namely Arthur, Percival, Tristan, Dagonet and Gawain whose upper left arm was tied round, as ever, with a green band.

Together they walked the route to the Palace of Whitehall, from where they would receive the final summons.

Arthur said nothing to his men, for they knew their duty. He strode ahead of the king, his eyes searching out hiding places and likely points for the ambush that he was certain Branok intended. Ravens cawed all around while they walked and then, suddenly...

They fell silent.

Arthur paused and readied himself, dropping a hand to the hilt of his sword.

And then he saw them. Six ravens coming in fast, bearing down on the party from the treetops. They made no call as they swooped.

Arthur removed his helm and held up his fist, calling a halt to the march.

'Away,' said Arthur under his breath, holding out his hand.

And that was all it took. The ravens recognised Charles's escort and wheeled away, cawing once more and returning to the trees. Here, Arthur was sure they knew, was a battle that they could not win.

'Why do we delay?' asked the king.

'A precaution, sire, but all is well,' said Arthur.

'Then lay on, Macduff,' said the king, his voice weary.

Branok's vision snapped back so that he once more saw the dull light behind his own closed eyelids. He breathed hard and looked about him.

If Arthur is here...

A hand took hold of his shoulder, and Branok staggered under its weight. He tried to turn but the force used against him was more than a hand could exert.

'Be at peace, Branok,' said Merlin, speaking into his ear so that the warlock could feel the old man's breath on his ear and neck.

'We must save him,' said Branok, still unable to turn.

'It is not a decision allotted to the likes of us, my friend,' he said. 'Arthur has decided to let this situation unfold naturally.'

'The King will be dead by sunset!' Branok objected and began to exert his own concentration. Slowly, ever so slowly, he turned to face Merlin. He saw only pity in the old wizard's face, and he understood.

'Arthur sent you,' said Branok.

Merlin nodded. 'But I would have come

unbidden, my friend. Nothing we can do here will benefit England or the Crown.'

'We can keep the blood alive, Merlin. Help Charles escape again,' Branok protested.

'And he will be recaptured. The people must learn this lesson for themselves. And as for the blood,' he took hold of Branok by both shoulders now, 'the blood will go on. Arthur has sent Kay and Ector abroad to watch over the king's children. They will return again one day, when the people will it.'

Branok said nothing. His spirit reached out for his familiars, but Merlin invaded his mind and suppressed his desire, broke his concentration.

'I cannot allow it, Branok. These wars have spilled too much blood. They end today,' Merlin said, and fury rose in Branok at how casually the words came, how untroubled Merlin seemed by Branok's efforts to contest his will. The older man dominated him, and Branok thrashed, his powers confined within the limits of his skull. Merlin shook his head and closed his eyes. Branok felt the ravens responding to the lightest touch of Merlin's will.

The familiars settled themselves atop the palace and cawed, watching the scene below.

Merlin turned Branok to face the scaffold once more.

'We will watch fate take its course, and you

will do nothing, then I will take you away from this place, and you can recover while the world moves on,' said Merlin. 'Nothing more can be done for Charles Stuart, by my hand or thine. He has sealed his own fate.'

Hours passed, and still the executioner could not be found. Knocking at his door went unheeded.

Desperate, discreet enquiries were made for volunteers and when they reached his ears, Arthur felt he owed his brother king the honour. He left his knights to guard the king's chamber, still fearful of Branok's meddling, taking only Tristan with him.

'Are you sure, Arthur?' said the knight. 'This cannot be God's will.'

'None of this is God's will, Brother,' Arthur replied as he pulled the executioners mask over his head. He watched as, after a moment of hesitation, Tristan did the same.

They walked out into the din of the crowds, and Arthur led the way up the steps to the scaffold, axe in hand. He frowned when he saw that a raven strode back and forth atop it, but the bird made no move against him.

Finally the time came, and King Charles I of England, Scotland and Ireland, still cloaked, came to stand atop the scaffold where he would surely die.

*

Branok visualised powerful arms reaching into Merlin's mind, tearing at the thoughts therein, beating at his will, but to no avail. He saw Charles appear before the crowd and called out to him, but his words were lost in the noise of the crowd. Someone raised his hand, and the crowd fell silent.

The king was speaking, but so far away Branok could not hear a word. He reached out to the raven to listen with its ears, and, perhaps in a moment of mercy, Merlin allowed it.

'I go from a corruptible to an incorruptible Crown, where no disturbance can be,' said King Charles.

And Branok never forgot it.

*

The king removed his cloak and handed it away. His hair tied up in a white nightcap, he lay upon the scaffold, his neck across the block.

Arthur breathed hard as the king looked up at him.

'I will offer up a prayer and signal when ready,' Charles said.

Arthur tried to reply but choked on the

words. He nodded and Charles faced forward once more, his hands on the block.

Arthur watched and waited as the king prayed, wondering if he was ever to be the instrument of the people and whether he would always suffer for it. His own death as king was not enough it seemed, he must take the life of another.

He watched, and he saw King Charles stretch out his hand.

Arthur hefted the axe and beheaded him with one clean blow.

The crowd groaned as one. A man passed out and dropped back into Branok, but Merlin held him steady.

'You see? England is still here, Branok,' said the old man's voice inside his mind. 'Now come away with me, and you may rest awhile. You have laboured hard these years past.'

'The words come easy for one whose boy still breathes,' said Branok.

'Is that so? And was Branok the Ravenmaster by my side on the field of Camlann when Arthur fell? Do you think the words came easy that day? You are young, Branok, at least in the eyes of the world. You will see how things come around, in time,' said Merlin.

Branok walked as though drugged, allowing himself to be steered through the dispersing crowd as the tears rolled down his cheeks, and the blood of King Charles I soaked into the sand on the scaffold.

Chapter Eleven

October 2019

Thick snow fell during the night. Arthur opened his bedroom curtains to survey his morning garden and looked out over an untouched canvas, save for the footprints of birds and squirrels. The trees beyond bore white coverings like ill-fitting tablecloths. Arthur lifted the sash window with some effort, sending a little avalanche over the brink. He ducked under the window and leaned out into the morning air, the dawn yet to break, and the amber glow of the estate lights illumining the snow drifts. Birds sang, but otherwise the world was silent, muffled by the broad white strokes of nature's brush.

A sudden impulse struck Arthur that he should like to go riding, and he dressed in a hurry. He opened the door to the landing with a gentle, gradual turn to avoid waking the rest of the household. He eased himself out and closed the door behind him. Only then did he notice a steaming mug of coffee on the small table by his door, accompanied by a pile of folded newspapers, bound with string. Arthur was fond of cutting open the parcel himself with a small knife.

Percival, thought Arthur as he reached down and took up the coffee, smiling.

He crept down to the drawing-room where he found a fire already burning in the hearth. Arthur sat in his chair while he drank his coffee, surveying first of all Excalibur and then the other weapons that hung around the room; a selection of cavalry sabres from down the centuries and assorted small arms, ranging from a pair of flintlock pistols to a Colt revolver. The ticking of a grandfather clock and the crackle of the fire were the only sounds. A pleasant tickle ran up Arthur's backbone as he basked in the warmth of the room.

He took his mug to the kitchen when he was done and pulled on a pair of boots before setting out across the virgin snow to the stables. He saddled his horse, Hunter, and led him towards the main gate. As he crossed the courtyard, the front door to the house swung open, and Percival stepped out onto the mat.

'A fine morning, sir,' he called.

Arthur told the knight he would not be long and thanked him for rising so early to meet his needs, that he appreciated it, as he had always done.

The last Arthur saw of him, Percival's cheeks were blooming red.

The sun was not yet up before Arthur mounted and spurred Hunter into a walk. He rode out on the grass verge at the side of the main road and, having reached the appropriate place, he urged the horse to cross so that they could head up the main drag towards the monument, a tall stone column with stairs running up the interior to the platform at the top, peaked with a green bowl. For the thousandth time, Arthur wondered whether it was actually hollow and, if so, what was concealed inside.

The snow hid the path, but both Arthur and Hunter knew the National Trust estate well, and the horse's hooves trod the bridleway without much guidance from his rider. Before long they were passing through a wide tunnel of trees, laden branches arching over them. Arthur took a deep breath of cold air and let his mind wander as the snow crunched beneath his mount, enjoying the mystic English autumn while he was at leisure to do so, for he knew there were dark days ahead.

A dog barked up ahead on the path, as yet unseen. Arthur looked for the animal, but the path bent round to the left and trees blocked his line of sight. Curious, and having no reason to do otherwise, Arthur rode on towards the sound.

Before he rounded the bend in the path, the dog, a Rottweiler, came round at a run. Hunter, no warhorse, whinnied and reared up. Arthur attempted to stay in the saddle, but his weak leg betrayed him. A moment of blind panic and he was slipping, falling and crashing down in the snow, coming to rest on his side.

A flash of pain in his bad leg caused Arthur to cry out. The Rottweiler padded over and sniffed at him, licking at his face.

'Jesus!' said a woman's voice.

Arthur rolled on to his back and was confronted by a woman in her mid-thirties, wearing a yellow raincoat and green wellington boots. Under her woollen hat, her brown hair hung to her shoulders. She held a looped leather leash in her hand.

'Stay still!' she said, and Arthur found he was obeying her command, which made his grimace give way to a smile.

'I'm intact,' he said, sounding far from certain even to his own ears.

'Stay still,' she said, an expression of worried concentration on her face, her brow wrinkling into neat little furrows.

'Where does it hurt?'

'Left leg,' said Arthur, 'but that's not unusual.'

She looked up to catch his eye, one eyebrow hitching in enquiry.

'War wound,' he said.

She nodded and said nothing as she knelt in the snow, commencing an examination of the leg.

Arthur, for the second time that morning, felt a curious tickling sensation run up his spine. He wondered whether she had taken the reference to his wound literally as he examined her face.

'Nothing obvious,' she said. 'How does it feel now?'

'It's easing off,' said Arthur. 'Really, I'm intact, I assure you.'

Arthur moved as if to stand, and she extended her hand. He paused momentarily, as if this simple touch of his leather-gloved hands to her wool-gloved ones would hold some great significance, then he grasped her hand, and the woman heaved him to his feet.

Arthur brushed the snow from his clothes and stepped to Hunter's side, rubbing the horse's neck and taking the reins.

'I'm ever so sorry,' said the woman.

'I'm grateful, lady, but there's no need for apology. You could not have foreseen it any more than could I,' said Arthur shaking his head. 'Don't think any more on it.'

She looked at him with a strange expression on her face. He thought she appeared bemused, and he was about to regain his saddle when a thought struck him.

'I wasn't expecting to find anyone else out before dawn, let alone a woman alone in the woods,' he said.

'Not alone,' she said, tipping her head towards the Rottweiler. 'Samson has my back.'

'Has your back?' asked Arthur.

'He's pretty off-putting to muggers and rapists. And horses apparently,' she smiled.

'You make a fair point,' he said, then added, 'Even so, it's rather early.'

'I work odd hours so I grab my chances while I can,' she said.

'Why odd hours?' he asked.

'I'm a doctor.'

'A physician?' asked Arthur, and she laughed.

'I don't get called that very often.'

Arthur felt his cheeks heating up despite the cold.

'Right, if you're sure you're all in one piece, I've got to head off and get ready for work,' said the woman.

Arthur nodded, finding it difficult to turn away from her.

He found her eyes captivating. It was as though they were drawing him in. The woman whistled for Samson, who was sniffing around in the undergrowth, and the dog trotted over. The trance broken, Arthur climbed up into the saddle and made himself comfortable for his continuing ride. He squeezed his heels, and Hunter took a few steps forward until Arthur reined him in.

The woman raised a farewell hand.

'Do call in to A&E if you find your leg's not ok,' she said in earnest.

'I will, Doctor,' said Arthur, sitting straight in the saddle.

'Caitlyn,' she said, smiling.

'Arthur,' he said. And then, as an afterthought, 'Perhaps we will meet again.'

'At odd hours in odd places,' she smiled, waved once more and walked back down the path towards the monument, Samson running ahead of her.

Arthur watched her go, his breathing fast and shallow, any pain quite forgotten for the time being.

Well, he thought. *Well, that was unexpected.*

'Am I interrupting?' said Merlin.

Arthur searched the treeline and saw the wizard in his long green coat, leaning against a makeshift staff, in the shade of an oak tree.

'Meddlesome goat,' said Arthur, and the wizard chuckled as he made his way through a patch of nettles to the main path.

'Are you following me, Merlin?' Arthur asked.

'My boy, I live to follow you,' was Merlin's solemn reply. 'Shall we walk?'

Arthur urged Hunter forward and Merlin accompanied him as they passed under the trees.

'I don't know where to start,' Arthur confessed after a few minutes of silence. 'How does one hunt down a warlock and his familiars?'

'Warily,' Merlin advised. 'Branok may be far stronger now. He had many long years to rejuvenate. I think he will not be overpowered as easily as he once was. And yet he is still a man. Think not of it as a hunt, but as a war with very few troops. What do we know about the enemy, of his strengths and weaknesses?'

Arthur mused on this for a time.

'Unless much has changed, he is but one man and with six supporters,' said Arthur. 'Six supporters who have no need of rest or sustenance, who feel no weariness and do not take sick. Skilled warriors and assassins, driven by his will and to no other end. They can disguise themselves as any living creature.'

Merlin nodded, whittling his staff with a small knife as he walked.

'And how do you bring such creatures to battle?'

'I do not know, Merlin. Speak plainly,' said Arthur.

Merlin sighed and took hold of Hunter's rein.

'Nigh on two millennia and still barely a thought between your ears. Devoted troops driven on by a determined general. How to give yourself the advantage, I wonder?' said Merlin, raising his eyebrows, his mouth hanging slightly open as though beginning to form the answer on his lips.

'Defeat the general and the troops will scatter,' said Arthur.

'Or in this case, dissipate, their bonds to this world broken,' said Merlin. 'The dead may finally sleep.'

'Branok *does* require shelter, rest and sustenance,' said Arthur.

'And he is a creature of habit,' said Merlin. 'A disciple of a craft akin to my own. If he dwells in a city or a town, it will not be his permanent lodgings, but if I know Branok, he will not wander as do I. He has not the care for the land, only its institutions. He will have a home, and we will seek him there.'

'And what do you suppose he is planning?' said Arthur. 'If one wished to save the monarchy in a land filled with many who wish to bring it down, where would one begin?'

'Two roads, he has before him, and both lead to loyalty,' said Merlin. 'He will persuade and coerce.'

'He has neither the imagination nor the inclination to persuade,' growled Arthur.

'History would bear you out on that, boy, for sure,' said Merlin. 'He will strike fear in the heart of the people and make them run back to the monarchy as frightened children run to their mothers.'

'But how?' said Arthur, despairing. Merlin's words made sense to him, and yet he felt no closer to an answer.

'Plague, war, assassination,' said Merlin, 'just off the top of my head.'

'Assassination,' said Arthur. 'Of whom? Those who drive the republican movement?'

'Aye, perhaps, perhaps,' said Merlin, 'but we can be sure of one thing, any action taken will be so that the people are forced to turn to the Crown for leadership and hope. Think back on the last war, Arthur, of how the Royal family stayed in London during the Blitz, of how the king would fly to meet with his troops around Europe and North Africa. They were never so beloved even if they did not direct the war effort themselves.'

Arthur said nothing, brooding on Branok's likely moves.

'By your arts, can you aid me further, Merlin?' he asked eventually.

The old man looked up at him, and Arthur saw the old twinkle in his eye.

'I have some ideas, boy,' said Merlin. 'Did you doubt it?'

'And I take it you won't be sharing them?

The wizard smiled. Arthur sighed, and Merlin swatted his leg.

'For now, boy, do as I do. Read the signs. Your own signs, in your own way,' said Merlin.

Arthur nodded.

'We will learn all we can before we quest after the Ravenmaster and his children,' he concluded, thinking of the stack of newspapers outside his bedroom door.

'Come, Merlin, let's head for home.'

Arthur rode with Merlin walking beside him and listened amused to the wizard wittering on about the trees they passed.

The old man came to a dead stop suddenly, bowing his head.

'Branok,' he said. 'He is near.'

Arthur hesitated momentarily, then realising the danger, he called out,

'Merlin!'

Arthur extended his hand, and the wizard allowed himself to be hauled up behind him. He wrapped his arms around Arthur's waist as Arthur spurred Hunter into a gallop.

'It may not be as you fear,' said Merlin quietly, the words resonating in Arthur's mind. 'He has never moved against you before.'

'The sword that strikes also parries,' Arthur shouted back over his shoulder. 'We have forgotten that all good generals know the best defence is a good offence.'

Arthur rode hard despite the snow, but Hunter kept his footing. They charged onward, crossing the main road, now marred by tyre tracks, and Arthur reined up only when he reached the driveway to his home.

The great gates were broken.

Chapter Twelve

Friday 3rd of September 1658 –
Palace of Whitehall
The Interregnum – England has no king.
Oliver Cromwell rules as Lord Protector

England, Scotland and Ireland have been without a monarch since 1649, and Cromwell has ruled since 1653. It is a time of hard principles and puritanism, when Catholics and other religious folk practise their faith in secret if they have any desire to go without persecution. A time of secret conflagrations, hidden chapels and priest holes, many that would never be discovered even after the need for them had passed.

Branok's lodgings within the Tower of London, provided by Charles I, were no longer available to him, and so he withdrew to his secret room within the Palace of Whitehall. He roamed the corridors, pale and gaunt, his hair unkempt and his long beard was grey. He walked unsteadily, drained and abused, exhausted from his constant efforts.

Safe within his chamber, he collapsed on his bed in the corner and rested for an hour, unable to sleep but lying with his eyes closed. He forced himself into a sitting position and ate the remainder of an earlier meal which still sat upon the table. His reserves bolstered as much as was possible without leaving the room again, Branok returned to work.

He mustered what remained of his energy, retrieved his besom from the corner of the room and began to sweep the floor in the centre of the room. The effort made his head swim, but he persisted until the area was devoid of dust and detritus.

He took a cedar flask and, pouring salt from within, he drew a circle with a nine-foot diameter, going over it twice until he was properly secured within it.

Using his old tinder box, Branok lit a blue candle.

'West, for water, the passage to the Underworld,' he intoned.

He lit a green candle, marking the north.

'North, for the Earth, to which the dead return.'

Next, a yellow candle.

'East, for the air, where the spirits reside.'

And finally, a red candle.

'South, for the fires in which we burn.'

Branok moved to the centre of the circle and drew his athame, his ritual knife. He pointed the tip of the blade towards the salt just beyond the west candle, where he had begun pouring and, closing his eyes, he turned slowly. He traced the circle, visualising his life energy flowing out along his arm and discharging through the athame's tip, forming a barrier between the world and the inside of the circle.

'The circle is cast,' said Branok, opening his eyes and sheathing the athame.

The room thrummed with power, or at least it felt as though it did to Branok, whose hands trembled and whose ears perceived a high-pitched whine emitting from some unknown source.

'I ask for the strength to sustain myself,' he said, as he collapsed to sitting. He crossed his legs and shifted the satchel that hung over his shoulder, the strap running across his chest.

Branok closed his eyes and waited, willing himself to reenergise, hopeful that the magick drawn in to the circle could provide.

His heart rate slowed, and his breathing came easier, and he knew he was ready to begin.

From within his robes he withdrew a lock of

hair, tied with a piece of black ribbon. He held it up on his open palm and began his incantation, picturing the face of the man from whose head the hair had been carefully, delicately snipped some months before. Branok pictured Oliver Cromwell, the Lord Protector of England, the crags and features of his face, and while he did so, he spoke words of malady, pestilence and sickness. He called down death and sent it out into the world, but not very far.

The door to Branok's chamber creaked open, and Joseph slipped inside, dressed in the attire of one of the serving staff within the palace. He paid little heed to Branok, who did not even acknowledge he had noticed the intrusion. Joseph moved to the table and drew out a quantity of herbs, dropped them into a small pouch and then, as quietly as he had entered, he departed, leaving Branok to his work.

Joseph took the most discreet path through the palace, passing silently down stairs until he neared the kitchens. In one of the lower corridors, he ducked into an alcove and stood to attention there as though he was a soldier lining the route to the throne room. Only a few minutes passed before he heard footsteps coming from the direction of the kitchens. A cook stepped into view as though she was expecting somebody waiting within. Martha held out her hand and Joseph, expressionless, dropped the pouch of herbs into her palm. She nodded once and left without a word, returning to the kitchens.

Joseph returned to the less functional, but more decorative, corridors of the palace and went about his daily tasks.

Each of the ravens had its duty. Martha stirred the herbs into a pot of soup and, when it was done, she prepared a bowl to be taken to the Lord Protector in his sickbed. Faith swept into the room and took it away without a word, proceeding at haste through the palace towards Cromwell's chamber. The guards opened the doors for her and once inside, the raven handed the tray upon which the bowl of soup was perched to the nursemaid sitting by the Lord Protector's side. Daisy stirred the soup and when the old man's head turned and his filmy eyes fell upon her, she sipped from one of the two spoons provided.

Cromwell lay on his back, his head propped up on a stack of pillows watching to see if his nursemaid would keel over from a dose of some poison, administered by some unknown assassin. Daisy did not die, and nodding his head, Cromwell allowed her to feed him.

He shivered, sweat dripping down his forehead as he slurped from the spoon. The soup escaped his maw and dribbled down his face. Cromwell swallowed, and for a time he felt well enough, but very soon he began to cough, his eyes widening and his brow furrowing as he frowned, his bowels beginning to cramp.

Daisy waited patiently, spoon poised, regarding Cromwell with dispassionate eyes. Slowly, ever so slowly, she fed him as much of the poisoned soup as he would take, just as she had done over the course of weeks and months, even while Branok directed his malice against the Lord Protector, this man who had taken up the mantle of leadership for a country that had overthrown and beheaded its king.

On Friday 3rd of September 1658, Oliver Cromwell, Lord Protector of the Commonwealth of England, Scotland and Ireland succumbed to his illness.

In 1660, Parliament invited Charles, son of Charles I, to return home to England having decided to proclaim him king. Escorted by Nathaniel and Isaac, Charles returned from the Netherlands and was crowned as King Charles II.

And Branok, sick as he was, paid homage.

In 1661 the ravens found their permanent lodgings in proximity to the home of their master. They became the famed ravens of the Tower of London.

Charles kept close counsel with the Ravenmaster, knowing, as his grandfather had known, that he owed Branok for his very existence and yet choosing, unlike his grandfather, to offer him due reward. The warlock took up lodgings within the White Tower, quietly and unacknowledged publicly, and yet close enough to keep watch and give counsel. The bloodline was restored, and the king had returned once more.

All was well, but Branok sat in his chamber high in the White Tower and his mind festered, unable to break away from rumination on things past, of the little boy in stiff leather boots, trying to walk despite the frailty of his legs. He remembered taking Charles I in his arms when he was still a small boy, of their many walks, rides and lessons. He pushed aside the bitter memories of the distance that grew between them during Charles's adolescence and the actions which led to the Civil War. Branok remembered the sight of the executioner's axe hacking Charles's head from his shoulders. He heard the groan of the crowd in every quiet moment, saw the blow every time he closed his eyes.

The people of London went about their business as the city sighed, and breathed, and grew. Branok looked out from the top of the White Tower and raged at the normality he saw all about him. They, like spoiled children, had their moment of rebellion, their time running the household and had failed. And now? The executed king's son sat on the throne and the House of Stuart was restored, but at what price to the people of England, thought Branok. At what price? Scarce any at all.

The new king seemed unconcerned with vengeance, but Branok, having dwelled on sickness and death and vengeance for the many long years of the Interregnum, could think of nothing else. He tasked the ravens with cultivating networks of spies and informers, sending them forth under the cover of night. They were his connection to the outside world while he sequestered himself in the Tower, and considered how best he could strike out at the people of England.

He brooded on the slow worrying away of Cromwell's health and spirit, the toll it had taken. Yet the more he considered it, the more convinced he became that he could do it again with the proper rest, and recuperation. If he hardened himself and drew all power to him. If he could muster all of his reserves and all of the aid that his arts could summon.

Chapter Thirteen

October 2019

Arthur dismounted and ran through the broken gates across the courtyard, limping as he went. The front door was open, and he charged inside, hands raised ready to shield himself or strike as need dictated.

He met no one in the lobby, but crashing and shouts came from upstairs. Arthur considered charging straight up there, but instead ran to the drawing-room. He found the door smashed from its hinges and lying between the armchairs by the fire.

It was as he feared. Excalibur was gone.

Cursing, Arthur snatched down a sabre and his Colt revolver, which he stuffed in his coat pocket, not worrying how easy it would be to draw.

He ran out of the room, unsheathing the sabre and hurling the scabbard to the floor as he burst up the stairs, ignoring the pain in his leg.

'Arthur,' he heard Merlin's call as he reached the landing, but ignored the wizard and ran on to aid whoever was under attack.

Tristan's body sailed from Arthur's open bedroom door and smashed into the opposite wall. The knight crumpled, and got to one knee, but before he could regain his feet, Daisy's foot crunched into his lower left ribs, delivered from a tremendous running kick as she followed him out of the room.

'Stand down!' roared Arthur, and Daisy's head snapped round. She eyed him, and a smile crept across her lips. Daisy took a fistful of Tristan's hair and raised her right fist, in which she held a dagger.

But Tristan struck out with his left arm, knocking her knife hand aside. He spun and thrust his right knee between her legs, knocking her off balance, and curled his right hand round her neck then followed the motion through to hurl her to the floor. She snarled as she slammed down hard.

Arthur ran forward, seeing that in taking the familiar down, Tristan had let her arm fly free. Arthur dived and, dropping the sabre, grabbed her wrist with both hands and bent it. Daisy cried out and dropped the knife.

To Arthur's left, Gareth's door flew open, and Joseph's colossal frame filled the doorway, his white eyes like unblemished moons. He stopped, surprised by the scene before him, which gave Gareth time to jump on his back, wrapping his arms around the familiar's throat. The bear of a man staggered back into the room and collapsed back on the knight.

Arthur seized Daisy's fallen knife and jumped to his feet.

'Where are the rest of us?' he shouted. Tristan, still grappling with Daisy, trying to secure her legs, didn't look up or answer.

'Arthur!' called Merlin again, and this time Arthur paid heed. He looked over the bannister and saw what he had missed before in his haste. Percival sat slumped behind the door in a pool of blood, his throat cut wide open, his dead eyes staring through the floor. Merlin stood over him, his back to the open front door.

Arthur took a step back.

'No,' he mouthed silently, gripping the knife ever tighter. He was mid-turn, ready to advance on Joseph and bury the dagger in the raven's heart when he caught a movement out of the corner of his eye. He looked back, but too late.

Martha stepped in through the open door, wielding Excalibur. She drew back the weapon, and by the time Arthur's gaze had returned to her she had swung the blade for Merlin's back.

The wizard sensed her and twisted away, but the blade hacked through his left arm like it was made of air.

The old man screamed as he fell across Percival's legs, the fallen knight's blood soaking into his white hair. Arthur's hands shook violently as he fumbled to switch the knife into his other hand.

He reached into his pocket, took hold of the Colt and hauled at it, but the barrel caught.

He wrenched at it and then, more deliberately, eased it free.

Arthur levelled the Colt and fired.

The revolver bucked in his hand as the boom filled the house. Arthur saw Martha reel backward as the bullet tore through her shoulder. She cried out as she was flung back out of the house into the snow. Arthur vaulted over the bannister and onto the stairs below. He ran down, but Kay appeared in the courtyard and snatched up Excalibur before Arthur reached the door.

'Arthur! Thank God!' he said as Arthur reached the ground floor. Martha lay on her back, clutching her shoulder, her body arching as she stared wide-eyed at the sky. Arthur thrust the revolver back in his pocket and cast the knife across the room.

'The others?' he called to Kay as he dropped to his knees at Merlin's side. The wizard clutched the stump of his arm, his disbelief and shock all too apparent. The arm itself lay lifeless on the floor, but the stump was sealed as though seared by a great heat. Excalibur's work sure enough.

'Percival is dead. Bors and Dagonet set out after you. Gawain is by the stables. As for the others, I cannot say,' Kay reported, breathing heavily. He stretched so that his back cracked, allowing the tip of Excalibur to cut into the blood-speckled snow. He stood over Martha, watching her writhe.

'Merlin,' said Arthur, for what else was there to say?

'He's still near,' Merlin gasped over and over again. 'Still...'

'Near,' said Branok. Arthur turned and saw the warlock standing behind Kay, his open hand outstretched as though reaching to grasp some unseen thing. Sir Kay made no move at all, seeming but a flesh statue of himself, Excalibur in his hand.

Branok closed his eyes, and all commotion stopped, save for shouts of surprise and the flapping of wings. Two ravens flew down the stairs, over Arthur's head and settled in the snow beside a third which stood now, quite unharmed, where Martha had been in agony just moments before.

Branok stepped forward and snatched Excalibur from Kay's hand.

He held the sword aloft as Arthur stood, hauling Merlin to his feet.

Merlin stumbled forward and closed his eyes, but Branok shook his head.

'Not any more, Merlin,' he said.

The three ravens formed a line before him, and Branok extended Excalibur so that it rested on Kay's shoulder, its edge cutting ever so slightly into the knight's neck.

'Let him go, Branok. He is an anointed knight of the country you claim to love so well,' Arthur growled.

'Your friend or your sword, Arthur,' said Branok. 'Choose.'

'Take it,' said Arthur without a second's hesitation.

'I would have your word that you will let us depart unopposed,' said Branok.

'Arthur, no,' gasped Merlin, seizing him by the shoulder.

'You have it, Branok. Spare his life and go,' said Arthur as Tristan and Gareth arrived by his side.

Branok lifted Excalibur and rested it across his own shoulder.

'You are no longer the powers that you were,' he said. 'I will show no mercy if you interfere with my plans, Arthur. And you, Merlin, your age has passed away.'

'I will not forget this, Branok,' said Arthur, but the warlock smiled.

'Remembering is all you are good for,' he said and turned to walk away. The ravens held Arthur, Merlin and the knights in their gaze until Branok neared the broken gate, then flew to him, perching on his shoulder and outstretched arm.

The warlock disappeared behind the high wall.

The knights ran forward as though a spell had broken, but when they reached the road, there was no sign of the Ravenmaster or his familiars.

Merlin dropped to his knees.

'This is the end of prophecy,' Merlin muttered. 'Here my vision fails. Excalibur is lost.'

Arthur clasped his mentor and friend by the shoulder, offering what comfort he could.

'It is but a sword, Merlin, there are greater losses to endure.'

Arthur called for the knights, and they returned to the house, filing into the lobby and gathering around Percival's fallen form.

Tristan stooped to dip his fingers in the cooling blood.

'I will avenge you, brother, I swear it,' he said, and none who heard him doubted it.

The knights built a pyre behind the house that evening and laid Percival upon it. Arthur himself lit a brand and set it amongst the kindling.

Arthur, Merlin and the remaining knights watched in silence as they bade farewell to their brother, too many memories over too many centuries for them to be spoken of aloud.

They drank together as the white clouds burst, and snowflakes fell once more across England.

Only when the wine was gone, and Percival was returned to dust, did Arthur address them.

'Our hiatus is at an end, brothers. Branok has struck first and struck hard, but little does he know he has caused the endgame to commence. Tonight, we mourn and we rest.'

Arthur reached down and grasped the hilt of the cavalry sabre that hung at his side and drew the weapon, holding it aloft.

'But tomorrow, we ride out.'

'Hear, hear,' said Tristan, drawing his weapon and thrusting it skyward. 'For Percival.'

The others drew their weapons in unison and echoed his words, but Merlin broke the circle, the remains of the arm of his coat sewn together. He leaned heavily on his staff and turned to look at them as he spoke.

'Aye, for Percival, but also for the land,' Merlin whispered, 'and for the realm.'

'For the people,' said Arthur.

Chapter Fourteen

December 1664

It began with the appearance of a comet, a feat that even Branok doubted he could achieve when he set about drawing it nigh. When first the beacon lit up the night sky, Merlin looked up along with the rest of the population, and he knew from the roots up that his apprentice was at work.

'That,' said Gaheris, 'is a sign of ill-portent.' And he was not alone in thinking so. Merlin saw awe, fear and wonder on the faces of Arthur and the remainder of the knights, who were lodging in inns and just about scraping a living by whatever methods they could now that the war was over and Charles II reigned.

'That,' said Merlin, 'is nothing of the sort,' for he could see what the others could not in the comet, 'or at least, not in the way everyone will assume.'

'Merlin?' said Arthur, recognising the wizard's tone.

'Is it a sign of ill-portent if you receive a letter informing you that your family will be slaughtered?'

'No, it's a threat,' said Arthur, understanding immediately.

Merlin pointed towards the comet.

Arthur said nothing.

'Branok?' asked Percival.

Nobody replied, and Percival did not ask again. He blushed, but nobody was looking to see.

'But why?' asked Bors. 'The wars are over, and the king is restored to the throne. Branok has achieved his desires.'

'Do you think that should Arthur be killed, I would be happy to forgive and forget just because a child of his regained the throne to carry on his bloodline? When the boy I raised had been murdered?' asked Merlin.

The knights made no reply, for many reasons, not least amongst them the memory of Arthur's first death from wounds sustained at the hands of Mordred at Camlann.

Merlin clasped his staff and leaned his forehead against the wood.

'I can feel him brooding, feel his malice. He is awake again. Mark my words – he *will* want revenge.'

'But against who?' asked Arthur.

'Against the people who overthrew their king. Against those who cleaved his head from his body,' Merlin replied, his face grim.

'Against me,' said Arthur.

Merlin shot him a sharp look, squinting in such a way that Arthur knew he was studying him, assessing his abilities as a pupil.

'That,' said Merlin, his voice low, 'will be the least of it, my boy'

July 1665

Arthur harboured no affection for London. He was unaccustomed to places such as these from the time of his youth. This, he pondered, bore little resemblance to his ideas for the capital city he had never had the chance to build, little in common with his vision of Camelot. London was a walled city in those days, and its four hundred thousand inhabitants dwelt in closely-packed buildings. Sewage sullied the streets, flies buzzed in the air, and smoke hung all around. Arthur passed folk who held scented handkerchiefs to their noses. He doubted it did them much good.

Even the old town houses abandoned by exiled Royalists during the Interregnum were divided up into tenements, packed with poor families. Beyond the walls, shanty towns had sprung up to accommodate the influx of people from the countryside, situated all too near the heaps of sewage that the rakers cleaned from the city streets only to dump them outside the walls.

That vision of hell, wrought by progress, somehow drew the people from the smaller towns, the villages and the countryside, and there, in the nation's capital, under his burning comet, Branok directed his malice. Hidden within the White Tower, he expended his will, casting enchantments and summoning dark powers to breed death at the heart of the city.

It began slowly, unnoticed. The Black Death, the plague, was a constant companion in those times, in part thanks to the warlock's early efforts to utilise his powers, encouraging the disease to spread, rather than conjuring it himself. In the city, where human excrement was thrown from windows to mingle with animal dung into the streets where the rats ran freely and flies buzzed overhead, sickness began to spread faster than ever before.

The authorities began house quarantines and ale houses were closed. Londoners were instructed to clean the streets in the front of their houses, but to no avail. The deaths mounted.

An exodus had begun.

Arthur's company rode towards the capital against the flow of constant traffic leaving the city. Even King Charles II fled Whitehall for Salisbury, fearing the disease. How little he understood the goings-on in his own kingdom, for Branok would not allow him to be touched by the plague, and the king did not suspect the Ravenmaster of any dark meddling.

Arthur led his men through the streets of London, and they observed the horrors first-hand: Xs painted on the doors of the sick, bodies heaped on carts by those calling 'bring out your dead' and the wily 'searchers of the dead', as they were known, women who made their living inspecting corpses to report the cause of death. Their purses jangled with coin, and not all of it obtained honestly, for who would not pay to hide the truth that the Black Death was upon their household?

Doctors visited the sick, wearing long all-covering robes, gloves and freakish white-beaked masks stuffed with herbs. Arthur shuddered as one nodded to him when their paths crossed, unable to see the man's eyes, and thinking him some hideous amalgamation of man and bird.

'We should get you out of here,' murmured Tristan, who stood at the king's side.

'I will not abandon my people,' said Arthur. 'There must be work we can do here. And we must find Branok.'

'You cannot aid your people if you fall sick yourself,' Tristan protested. 'Go back to the countryside, sire. I will stay here with half of our brothers.'

But Arthur would hear none of it.

Arthur and the knights spent their days and often their nights doing whatever they could to be of assistance to the locals. They fetched water, they cleaned streets, they tended the sick, but all the while Merlin wandered the streets, reaching out for Branok until one day in the late summer, a raven flew down from a rooftop and perched upon his shoulder.

Merlin flinched, fearing the bird would peck out his eye, but it tightened its grip and simply sat, waiting for the wizard to be still. Merlin turned, cautiously, stretching his neck away from the bird as he did so, to look. The raven cawed, which made the wizard jump, then tilted its head.

'Bloody bird,' said Merlin as his heart began to slow again, convinced the raven was actually smiling, despite the rigidity of its bill.

It leaned towards him, and Branok's voice issued in a whisper like a drop of fluid squeezed from a pipette.

'Are you coming to see me, Merlin?'

Merlin shivered and frowned at the bird.

'If I knew where you were,' he snapped at the raven. A woman on the other side of the street stopped, folded her arms across her chest and hurried away from him. Merlin watched her go and then stepped into a quieter side street.

'Come to the Tower, and I will meet you there,' said Martha in her bird form. She cawed again, once more startling Merlin. He would have sworn that the raven cackled as she flew away east.

A mist enveloped the Tower of London, and Merlin could see nothing of it except for the tops of its towers and battlements, like the peaks of mountains poking through a layer of grey cloud. His footsteps echoed as he approached, warily, for he had no status that merited doing so, at least as far as the government and those who watched over the Tower were concerned. He stopped some way before the gate and reached out to Branok with his mind. He recognised his apprentice's reciprocal touch and sat upon a low wall, awaiting the younger man's appearance or a summons to him.

Finally a cluster of figures emerged through the gate, two separate files of three people each on either side of a lone man, dressed in fine clothes, all dark and with a silver tracery of thread upon them. As they drew near, Merlin saw the escort for what they were, the ravens, and it was no surprise to him.

Branok's familiars dispersed in the mist, and the man himself walked slowly towards his mentor, leaning upon a cane, his wide-brimmed black hat set at a jaunty angle.

Merlin, in his raggedy coat, leaning heavily upon his staff, with leaves and morsels of food hanging in his beard, swung his legs out, dropping his heels back against the stone wall that was his seat, like a child asked to wait patiently. He offered Branok a slow nod of the head, wary as to how this meeting would unfold. After all, the last time they had met, Merlin had held Branok entranced while the king's head was lopped from his shoulders.

'Merlin,' said Branok as he came to a stop before him.

'You've done very well for yourself, I see,' said Merlin. 'Such fine clothes, such elaborate lodgings.'

'Each to their own,' Branok replied.

'Are you going to kill me, boy?' asked the wizard. 'Let's come to the point, so if we are going to move beyond it, we can do it all the sooner. I have other business.'

'Do you think I could, if I wanted to?' asked Branok.

'Nothing is impossible, but I'd caution against the attempt,' said Merlin, 'though the state of this city is evidence enough that your powers have grown considerably since last we met.'

Branok began to speak, but Merlin held up his hand and both men felt the effect. Merlin, reassured, continued.

'No, boy, I do not wish to know how you have achieved this malignant mischief. You are already a sorrow to me.'

Branok closed his mouth and stared thoughtfully at Merlin, as though deciding whether to go on the offensive or defer to his mentor, as he had as a child.

'I could feel you searching for me,' said Branok, 'and now you have found me.'

'You have presented yourself, rather. No false modesty, boy,' said Merlin.

'It comes down to the same thing in the end,' said Branok.

Merlin nodded.

'Indeed. Well, to it, then,' he cleared his

throat. 'It's time to put an end to the epidemic. You've wreaked havoc enough. Had your revenge. How many thousands must die to avenge one man's life?' His words were gentle, the question genuine.

'I'll know the figure when I happen upon it,' said Branok, with a sneering tone that, to Merlin, seemed as though he was trying too hard to appear disaffected; an affectation.

'The people you are killing had little to do with Charles's death, you know? The rich, the nobility, everyone of consequence has fled the city now. You are culling the weak and the needy, Branok.'

The warlock made no reply.

'I know full well you are hurting, Bran,' Merlin said as he stood. He stood before Branok and rested a hand on his shoulder, meeting the warlock's eyes, 'but *this* is not the way.'

His former pupil held Merlin's gaze for as long as he could, then he looked down at his boots.

'Wrong or right, it is of no consequence any more. My well runs dry. I can goad the plague no longer, so either way, you will get what you wish. Less people die by the day,' Branok muttered.

'That's a good thing, boy,' said Merlin, ducking down to try to regain eye contact as he carried on speaking, 'I can only imagine your pain at losing Charles, but it was fated. It was always his doom. This country, this England, it means far more than any one man's life. And if you taught him anything, I am sure he would not wish you to claim retribution by hurting innocent people.'

Branok said nothing and for a time, Merlin thought he had seen reason, but then his pupil spoke again.

'This England is one man. Nothing else matters. When they speak of England in the colonies, or on the Continent, they do not speak of her green fields or her lice-infested populace, they speak of the king. "What will the king do next?" That bloodline is sacred to me, Merlin. I have helped to shape a nation far more than you ever did. What is your legacy, a dead king reborn to do nothing? Embellished history passed on into storybook legend? The people of this country rose up and struck down what was divine, and they must pay weregild until I deem it otherwise. This city will rue the day it allowed the blood of the House of Stuart to run in its streets.'

He shrugged off Merlin's hand and stepped back.

The wizard sighed and clasped his staff.

'You are not yet so strong that I could not intercede, as I have before,' said Merlin.

'Do not think I forget it, old man,' said Branok, and once more Merlin shivered as his pupil stalked back towards the Tower, and his familiars emerged from the mist.

'The bloodline is renewed. A king of the House of Stuart rules once more. Be content. You have taken your pound of flesh, and taken your revenge. All of your enemies are dead.'

Branok stopped and turned, smiling.

'Not all my enemies, Merlin. Your time will come, and so will Arthur's. When I am ready.'

He turned and began walking again.

'There will be no more chances, Branok. If you strike out at the people again, we will come for you,' Merlin cried after his retreating pupil, who paid him no heed at all.

Merlin stood there long after the company had passed away through the Tower gates, He stared at the fortress, his heart aching for the boy he had once thought could guide England in his place when finally he took his final sleep.

Eventually, slowly, he turned and walked back into the city, the sound of cawing ravens fading behind him.

Chapter Fifteen

October 2019

Delaying, Arthur considered, may have been a mistake. After all there was a chance, albeit slim, that Branok and his familiars had left some sort of tracks as they retreated through the woods or along the roads. But what then? Further disgrace and defeat for whosoever should catch them?

No, he decided, better that his knights had slept for a while in their own beds and could set out refreshed with whatever aid Merlin could offer them.

He joined the company at a solemn breakfast, eaten largely in silence. The men tucked into coffee, eggs, bacon and sausages, and it was only when the last of them had laid down his cutlery that any of them spoke.

'This hunt will be nigh on impossible, sir,' said Tristan. 'Advanced with all zeal, we still have no idea where Branok may be hiding or how we can discover the same. And if any of us should find him, what stops him from holding us frozen as he did to Kay last night so that his ravens may peck us unceasing?'

Murmurs of agreement from around the table, and all looked to Arthur.

'I have no more answers in this matter than do the rest of you, but a few facts are clear. Percival is dead and must be avenged, and Britain is under threat once more by…' here he looked at Merlin, 'one of our own. We have a duty to prevent whatever mischief he is planning and a duty to Percival.'

'But how to go about it, sir?' asked Kay.

'Branok is ever watchful of the bloodline himself, so he will not have strayed far from London unless my reckoning is out. We must consider where we would strike if we were in his shoes, and see if we can open up some lines of enquiry which we can all pursue,' said Arthur. 'I can suggest nothing more than what we came up with at council the other night.'

'If *I* might interject, I might have *something* to offer, you know,' Merlin snapped, prompting disguised smiles around the room, except from Arthur.

'It will do no good to hunt down the familiars while Branok yet lives. The ravens are not the first familiars he has conjured, and they will not be the last if any of them should fall. He will just summon more spirits to aid him. No, it is Branok himself that we must hunt to put a true end to these proceedings. The familiars must be prevented from carrying out their master's plan, but it is the master who must be located and stopped,' said Merlin. 'I am our best chance of finding him.'

'How so?' asked Kay.

'I am attuned to the boy,' said Merlin. 'I have known him since he was a child, some five hundred years ago, and I taught him much of what he knows. I sensed his arrival yesterday, and though I know not how close I must be to do so, that is something that can be put to the test.'

'He will be,' said Bors, almost lazily, 'at the Tower.' He slurped from his coffee and sighed contentedly when he had drained it.

'Why do you say that?' asked Arthur.

'Beasts like their own holes,' said Bors.

'Is that all you can contribute?' said Tristan, but Merlin looked thoughtful.

'It's like criminals. Do they ditch their old lives to start afresh? No! They sleep on friends' sofas and get picked up in old haunts. Branok is not so very different. He's spent what, 300 years in the Tower?' said Bors.

'Nearer 400,' said Merlin.

'Right, 400,' nodded Bors, as though he had said so in the beginning. 'It's like a fellow released from prison after a long stretch. After twenty years a man can be at odds with the world outside, finding it strange and unfamiliar. How well did we first cope after our long slumber? We were not as fortunate as Branok, our old haunts were long gone. He will be at the Tower, I say, and if not there, then other places that we should be able to list.'

The others sat in silence after this outburst drew to a close, each of them having initially marvelled at Bors's idiocy, before realising that he might just have a point.

'Perhaps that is the place to begin,' said Arthur.

'Aye, perhaps,' said Bors as he reached across to steal a slice of toast from Tristan's plate.

After breakfast everyone set about packing whatever they would need on the road, while Arthur and Merlin worked on a list of Branok's likely haunts. They decided on an order and made copies for each of the men, starting with the closest to London.

'The list is not so long,' said Merlin.

'And yet more than any could search fully in a lifetime,' said Arthur.

They pushed back their chairs and went in search of the knights. All were assembled in the lobby beside a line of suitcases, atop each of which lay a single long leather case.

'How many guises you all have assumed,' laughed Merlin. 'When first I saw you all as a body, you were clad in armour with swords hanging from your belts, grim-faced and eager.'

'And now?' said Tristan, quietly.

Merlin, less acquainted with the tropes of the age, stuttered, but Arthur helped him out.

'Well-groomed investment bankers,' he smiled, and they returned it with affection, all save Tristan, who frowned and folded his arms across his chest.

'No matter the trappings, you are still knights of Britain, and I know your hearts to be true,' said Arthur. He took the pile of papers from Merlin and handed one to each of the men.

'These are the areas where Branok may be haunting, if Bors is correct,' said Arthur.

'Which he is,' said Bors.

'By some miracle,' said Tristan.

'Quiet,' said Kay before Bors could make his retort.

'I will stay here for a few days and play the puppet master for our friends in parliament, in business and with the police. I will also ensure that the line of succession for our various businesses and charities is in place before I embark on what could well be our last task,' said Arthur.

'Tristan, Ector, Kay and Lucan, you will go to the London house to ready it for our arrival. Make sure all is secure and that there have been no intrusions there. Bors and Dagonet, you will escort Merlin to Wiltshire when we are done here. Scout out the area, drive around all of the nearby towns and villages. Spend a day or so searching out the woodland until Merlin is content, then do the same around where Branok was living when he was mentoring Charles. Once Merlin is happy, rendezvous with the rest in London. Bedivere can join us in London when his current work is done. Kay and Lucan will go to Edinburgh with Merlin if and when he is satisfied Branok is not in London. All clear?'

'Understood,' said Bors, and the others nodded assent. All except Tristan.

'That leaves nobody to stay at your side, sir,' said Tristan.

'I require time to meditate and prepare,' said Arthur. 'Branok will not strike here again.'

Tristan began to reply, but Arthur held up his hand and the knight fell silent.

'I will stay here, alone, and put my affairs in order. Now, you have your tasks. Be bold, but not foolhardy. And listen to Merlin until it no longer pays to listen,' he smiled and rested a hand on the old wizard's shoulder, but Merlin shrugged him off, harrumphing.

Eventually only one suitcase remained in the lobby, and two cars pulled out of the estate. Arthur listened to the sound of their engines fading and then returned to the quiet sanctum of his home, closing the thick oak door behind him. No sound, but for the ticking of a grandfather clock.

Arthur stared at the blood-stained hardwood floor of the lobby, lost in thought for a time.

He wandered the ground floor, room to room, taking it all in and perhaps saying goodbye in his own way. He eschewed the drawing-room and moved slowly up the stairs to move between the bedrooms, looking out over the woods from each of the windows, and closing the doors behind him. Finally he returned to the drawing-room and took a seat by the hearth, devoid of fire and warmth. Arthur listened to the ticking of the clock for a time then moved to his desk and began to call his friends, in high places and low, seeking what he could find.

Chapter Sixteen

Monday 5th of November 2019

Arthur woke on the morning of Bonfire Night, the 414th anniversary of the capture of Guy Fawkes, and found that he had slept far later than intended. The hours spent making fruitless calls and sending equally fruitless emails had taken its toll, it seemed.

He dressed and, passing his suitcase in the hall, made coffee then put two slices of toast under the grill while his drink cooled. He slathered the bread with salty butter and sat alone at the small table in the kitchen while he ate, his peace disturbed only by the sound of crunching. The house had the still atmosphere that precedes some long journey into the unknown, and Arthur could feel the hairs standing up on the back of his neck.

He fetched his coat, boots and cane then walked across the snow to the kennels, releasing his hounds, Cynbel and Drust. As soon as the door was open, they burst from their warm lodgings, circled his feet and leapt up at him with their tails wagging. He tousled their furry heads, patting their sides and urging them on as he made for the main gate.

Arthur walked the very same path he had ridden out upon on the morning of the attack on his home. The snow crunched underfoot as he walked, and once they were away from the road, Arthur let the dogs roam farther ahead. He walked with his head down, watching his cane poke holes in the snow, thinking of Percival, and of the others they had lost as the centuries passed by.

He wiped a patch clear on a fallen log beside the path and sat, looking across the tree-lined field at the centre of the estate, in the middle of which grew an imposing oak tree. A light wind blew, and Arthur closed his eyes, leaning on his cane, trying to remember the clean air and vigour of his youth. He tried to conjure the images of his fallen knights and of Mordred, the son whom he had killed hundreds of years ago, but it was as difficult as trying to recall a dream; they remained just on the edge of his vision and slipped away into dark water.

He opened his eyes and saw the hounds circling a Rottweiler on the field, but before he realised what this meant, the lady spoke beside him.

'Have I caught you napping?' Caitlyn said, eyebrows raised in mock earnestness.

'Just remembering,' he said, finding he was excited and comforted by her presence. 'Take a seat.' He cleared a spot beside him. She perched on the log, nestling a thermal cup between her hands.

'Coffee?' he asked.

'Hot chocolate. Don't tell my nutritionist,' she replied as she watched the dogs play.

'So what were you remembering?' asked Caitlyn.

Arthur smiled, but she persisted.

'What? Is it a secret?' she teased.

'I was thinking back on younger days and of some people who fell behind on the journey,' he said. 'Lost friends and family.'

She nodded, her playful smile replaced with a slightly strained expression, which Arthur recognised as empathy.

'Anyone in particular?' she said, softer now, more cautious.

'I lost a lifelong friend only yesterday afternoon,' said Arthur, surprised to hear himself choking on the words. Caitlyn made no reply for a moment then shuffled closer and wrapped an arm around him and leaned her head on his shoulder.

'I'm sorry,' she said.

The two of them sat motionless, their breath hanging in the air before them. He caught the scent of her perfume, and he shuddered, but pleasantly. She felt the movement and looked up at him, and when she saw he did not look discomfited she leaned on him again.

'Can I ask you a strange question?' he said.

'If I can hit you if I don't like it,' she said.

'Do you enjoy your life?' said Arthur, still leaning on his walking stick, one hand atop the other.

She paused, thinking before answering. He appreciated that.

'For the most part. I have a lovely home, a supportive family, and my career is going well. But who doesn't have frustrations and things that could be improved?' she said.

He nodded and made no reply.

'Do you?' she asked, sitting upright and sipping her chocolate.

Arthur was not sure how to answer.

'I'm not sure that the question has any meaning for me, in all truth,' he said. 'I had a life when I was young, but this new phase,' he paused. 'I have everything a man needs to survive, and yet I am forever shackled by the obligations and promises of my youth, although I am now ill-equipped to fulfil them. I suppose that doesn't make any sense,' he said, laughing without humour.

'Were you a child star or something?' she teased. 'Are you Hayley Mills? Macauley Culkin, maybe?'

At this, Arthur laughed out loud.

'You're not entirely wrong actually,' he said. 'It's not a bad analogy. I sometimes feel a little left behind. I don't look so very old, but some aspects of life stop advancing, tastes and morals get frozen at certain points, and I can't seem to move beyond them.'

'I know what you mean. I haven't listened to new music since 1998,' said Caitlyn.

'That's exactly it,' said Arthur, 'but across the board. Music. Food. Manners. Clothing. They all seem foreign to me now.'

'That's just getting old,' said Caitlyn, 'and part of getting old is accepting that you like what you like and not being beholden to fads and fashions.'

'What if what you like is considered outdated?' said Arthur.

'Unless you're going to get arrested for it, I wouldn't worry,' she said, and Arthur thought of Agravain, sitting in his cell even as the two of them sat upon a log on this crisp autumn morning.

Arthur sighed.

'You seem lonely,' said Caitlyn.

'I am,' said Arthur. 'I've been living to fight for a cause for so long that I can scarcely remember what I wanted from life.'

'Well, what do you want?' she asked softly. He felt her shuffle closer, the heat of her against his leg and arm.

'Peace, I suppose, and the same opportunities as everyone else,' he said.

'Opportunities to do what?' she asked.

To live out my days. To grow old and die, he thought. *To rest.*

'To enjoy my home. To walk the woods. To spent my days following my passions or doing nothing at all,' he said.

'To retire? I hear you,' she smiled. 'I have to wait longer than you do, so you'll get no sympathy from me, buddy.' She elbowed him, grinning as she did so.

'What's stopping you?' she asked.

'I could walk away, but I feel a duty to carry on,' he said, and he sighed, feeling as though he was finally unburdening himself, even if they were talking around the true topic.

'I'm defined by what I do,' said Arthur.

'My father had the same problem after he left the army. He ended up joining the police. After he retired, he always felt at a loose end, as though he had been taken out of the game,' said Caitlyn.

Arthur looked at her, this child of the age, who was knocking his problems back at him so simply. What could she understand of a man who had walked this island before the Romans left? Who had been presented with the Victoria Cross by Queen Victoria herself? Whose food had changed from roast dormouse to Pop-Tarts? How could she ever understand that a man who has lived through centuries leaves a little of himself in each? And yet Arthur suspected that perhaps she could.

'He adjusted eventually,' said Caitlyn. 'All it takes is time. And keeping occupied.'

'Perhaps,' said Arthur. 'I've been bending your ear, I'm sorry.'

'It's natural when you lose a friend, especially if it was unexpected?' she said.

'It was,' said Arthur. 'I didn't see it coming at all. Not now, in this place, after all we've been through.'

She leaned against his shoulder again.

'If you ever need to talk. Or you need help keeping occupied, I'm more than willing,' said Caitlyn, sounding like a girl asking a boy to dance for the first time.

Arthur turned, hooking his knee up on the log so he could face her properly.

'I'd like that,' he said then, 'though I have to deal with my friend's estate before I can think of socialising again. I'm going away for a while.'

Caitlyn pointed right along the path.

'I live down there in Hunter's Cottage. Do you know it?'

'Down the left fork, down a steep path?' said Arthur.

'That's the one,' said Caitlyn. 'Drop by and leave me a note if I'm not in? I can't be doing with phones.'

They stayed a while longer, but Arthur grew ever more aware of the time and finally bade her farewell. He called for his hounds and, reluctantly, with much cajoling and not a little harshness added to Arthur's calls, Cynbel and Drust came to heel.

He walked back to the house, but this time Arthur walked with his head held high and his back straight, renewed in purpose. This would be his final quest, however it ended.

That evening Arthur took a taxi to the nearest train station. He found himself a window seat so that he could watch the countryside go by and think during the brief trip south into London. The tide of commuters at Euston station set his head spinning, so he sought escape by jumping into a black cab, putting off the time when he would need to face Merlin and his knights again. He stepped down to the pavement on the Embankment and walked west along the Thames in the lamplight, the waters shimmering as they ran eastward beside him. Fireworks banged and sparkled in the distant skies as Arthur approached the Houses of Parliament. He looked up at Elizabeth Tower and listened as Big Ben tolled inside, as the clock struck 8pm, and explosions of colour went off behind the buildings, filling the air with magic.

A fluttering overhead drew his attention, and Arthur saw a raven perch upon the statue of Boudicca just ahead of him on the left. The bird looked at him and cocked its head.

Arthur clasped his lapels together and, suitcase in hand, he walked back the way he had come.

Chapter Seventeen

The Great Fire of London - 1666

'Enough,' said Arthur, his soot-stained face running with sweat, his breathing laboured in the oppressive heat. Smoke swirled all around and the flames licked at the night sky.

His knights broke away from tearing down a house to create a firebreak. Arthur threw down the beam he had been dragging and stormed away from the site of the destruction in such a way that all of his men knew full well that his temper had broken.

Away from the searing heat, Arthur turned to them all and shouted,

'This is him. Branok, it must be. He drives the fire onward with his malice!' Arthur roared.

'We cannot know that for sure, sir,' said Tristan.

'Cannot know it? I know it! I know it, well enough,' said Arthur. 'First the plague and now fire. Branok will not be happy until the people have paid for what they did to his boy,' he said.

'And who would not wish to avenge a son,' said Kay.

Arthur stormed forward and grasped Kay by the shoulders.

'Charles was not his son! No matter how deluded he may be about him, we cannot allow ourselves to forget it. Branok is deluded beyond our reckoning. Fanatical about what, a bloodline passed down through the ages? Are not all bloodlines? There have been countless injustices in this world, if you can call the execution of Charles an injustice at all, but it was not the greatest of them. Are the people of England to pay for it forever?' His temper cooled somewhat, and he released Kay, lightly patting the man's cheek with his open palm.

'No, Brother. This is a madman's folly, not a parent's grief. Abandon your work here, and join me. Our hands would be better put to destroying the arsonist than putting out the flames,' he said.

'Return to your lodgings and arm yourselves. We make for the Tower.'

Attended by Gareth and Tristan, Arthur strode through the streets, busy with people packing their possessions and moving westward to escape the flames which seemed to engulf buildings faster than any could pull them down. Two nights the fire had raged now, leaping from one building to the next in those cramped and crowded streets.

When all were armed, Arthur's company left the pair of taverns in which they had been lodging to find Merlin, unsummoned, waiting in the street.

'Are you ready?' he asked of them.

'We are. It is time,' said Arthur.

'Then follow me,' said Merlin.

The wizard led Arthur, Gareth, Tristan, Gaheris, Lamorak, Galahad, Bedivere, Percival, Bors, Kay, Ector, Lucan, Dagonet, Gawain, Geraint and Agravain, with the knights clearing the path ahead as they travelled south towards the river. Once there, Merlin shepherded them aboard a small craft, which Arthur supposed he had purchased, stolen or commandeered, but thought better of questioning the old man. The company crowded into the boat, Merlin pushed off, and they began to row eastward. The night sky glowed red and yellow, with banks of smoke carrying westward in the wind. The flaming city skyline struck fear into Arthur's heart, knowing all too well what power was behind it.

The boat made good progress down the unusually quiet river until they drew close to the Tower of London on the north bank. The craft steered, seemingly with no human intervention, towards Traitor's Gate. The watergate was down and troops stood guard, but Merlin raised his hand, and when the gate began to slowly rise, Arthur could see no reaction from the men guarding it, as though they had been turned to statues. He marvelled, as always, at Merlin's arts, feeling not a little uncomfortable, but he steeled his heart as they passed through the gate and into the Tower, Merlin seeming to cast all obstructions aside and holding any they came across in place with the force of his will.

King Arthur and his knights stood by St Thomas's Tower and gathered their wits before moving on. They passed like ghosts through the passages until the White Tower stood before them, menacing and majestic for all its ancient crudity.

Merlin closed his eyes and reached out both hands. With a twitch of his fingers, the Yeoman Warders thereabouts stood insensible, and the company advanced upon the White Tower.

Arthur had never been inside before, and yet he had heard the legends, and he stared harder at the mound beneath the Tower than he did at the fortress itself, wondering if it were true indeed, as the legends told, that the head of Bran,

King of Briton was buried beneath the hill facing towards France, staving off invasion. If so, he had done a poor job, thought Arthur, given that the building standing over him had been built by William the Conqueror, the victorious invader from Normandy.

'The efficacy of kings,' he muttered.

'Sire?' said Tristan, and Arthur shook his head.

'No matter,' he said, as they drew close to the Tower steps.

'No farther,' said a voice from above the main door to the Tower.

Arthur looked up and saw a raven perched above his head. The king made no reply to the bird, thinking he had imagined the sound.

The bird cocked its head and peered down at him.

'No farther,' it cawed.

Arthur drew his sabre on instinct, feeling vaguely ridiculous as he tried to come up with a reply to the bird.

An explosion beside him, and the bird took flight as a shot ricocheted from the stone wall. Arthur turned to see Bors lowering his pistol. The knight shrugged.

Arthur turned to follow the raven's flight and started when he saw it land at the end of a line of five people, all facing directly towards them, clad entirely in black, their faces pale. The raven fluttered its wings and suddenly was gone, replaced by a young woman, similar in appearance to the other five.

'No farther,' said Daisy, her words echoing around the Tower courtyard.

Merlin reached out and cast his enchantment upon them, but all six of the ravens drew their swords in unison and began to walk slowly forward, their eyes fixed on Arthur's company, accompanied by the cacophony raised both by the fire and the shouts of the Londoners outside the Tower.

Merlin opened his eyes.

'I cannot hold them off by my will alone,' said Merlin. 'They do not have living minds such as that of man.'

'Lamorak, Gaheris, with me. The rest of you, hold them off,' said Arthur. 'Go.'

'For England!' growled Galahad as he drew his sabre and led the others in a charge down the steps to meet the ravens in combat.

Merlin turned his attention to the door. He moved close and leaning on his staff, he closed his eyes and concentrated. Arthur watched as his thirteen knights charged towards the slowly walking ravens, none of whom seemed in the least concerned about the assault.

The two sides came together in a clash of

steel and thudding bodies. The first strokes were parried and the assailants pressed on as the ravens wheeled away, darting left, striking right, stabbing, slashing and feinting almost faster than the eye could perceive. None could stand up to such an onslaught that the ravens offered, none save for these knights of legend, brought back from the dead for this very purpose. Arthur's men parried every blow and bore the force of the riposte. They took the measure of their enemies, who drifted like smoke and struck like lightning under the failing moonlight.

Joseph seized Tristan by the throat with his off-hand.

'You have the blood of King Charles on your hands. Where is your hood now?'

Tristan drove his knee into Joseph's hip and struck down with his pommel, smashing it into the top of the raven's head. Joseph grunted and staggered, releasing his grip, but even as Tristan leaped to take advantage, the raven had recovered, and once more drove Tristan back.

So it was with all of them, only their instincts and their skill keeping them alive against these demons or ghosts or whatever they were that Branok had summoned.

Arthur heard a noise behind him and turned to see the door to the White Tower swing open.

A dazed yeoman warder stood holding it for them and, with one final look back, Arthur said a prayer for his men as he, Merlin, Lamorak and Gaheris entered the Tower to commence their search.

Even then the Tower was centuries old, a fortress of stone and wood, its many tapestries and adornments failing to belie the simplicity of an earlier time. The Tower now housed a vast quantity of gunpowder.

'He is here,' said Merlin as they moved carefully through the White Tower.

Wordlessly they searched room by room, Merlin casting open locked doors and incapacitating all they encountered with a wave of his hand.

And then, high up in the Tower, behind a modest door, which all but Merlin had failed to notice, they found their quarry.

The door swung open to reveal a modest cell in which stood a bunk and a table. Piled books were stacked here and there. Bones and plants, candles and sigils were in evidence, but nothing so indicative of the arts practised within as Branok himself, arms raised and eyes closed, standing within a circle of salt in the centre of the room. Gaheris and Lamorak dashed forward and seized the warlock by his arms, and Arthur drove him back against the wall of the cell, his left arm across Branok's throat and his sword raised in his right hand.

Merlin crossed the room.

'No, stay back,' said Branok, but Merlin laid his hand upon his pupil's brow.

'An end to this,' said Merlin, and Branok ceased resisting, his eyes vacant, his mouth hanging open and his tongue lolling forward like a saliva-smeared toad.

'Sleep now, and strike all thoughts of vengeance from your dreams,' said Merlin. Branok's body sagged, forcing the knights to adjust their positions.

'Lay him on his bunk,' said Merlin. 'He will offer us no more strife for many a year.'

'Will we not kill him?' said Lamorak and instantly regretted it when he saw the fury in Arthur's eyes.

'No, I would not have it so, after all,' said Lamorak in answer to himself. 'He is defeated and defenceless.'

'And to kill him would be murder,' said Arthur. 'Think before you speak.'

'We will do to him what was done to me for many long years,' said Merlin. 'He will not thank me for it, but it did me no lasting harm. All of you out of the room now.'

Arthur, the chastened Lamorak and Gaheris

drew back into the corridor with Merlin following on behind.

'Go and aid the others. His familiars will yet be fighting,' he said. 'I will conclude our business here.'

'Do as he says,' said Arthur, but as the knights ran to aid their brothers, he stood back and watched the wizard at work.

Merlin closed the door, and he twisted his fingers as though there were an unseen key in an unperceived keyhole in the door. Arthur thought he heard a lock snap home. Merlin looked as though he were lifting and then setting in place a wooden beam across the door. He stood back and lowered his head and began to speak in an ancient tongue of the island, calling forth some power that Arthur could not guess. As Merlin spoke, the concept of the door wavered in Arthur's mind, seeming to merge with the stone, and then, between blinks, it was gone, replaced with a blank wall. Merlin did not break off chanting for some minutes yet, and only when he was clearly finished, panting and steadying himself on his staff, did Arthur step forward, reaching out to touch the stone where the door had been.

But as he did so, he withdrew his hand, unable to recall why it was outstretched. Why was he approaching the wall as though to touch it?

Merlin's weak laugh distracted him, and Arthur saw Merlin beckoning him away from the wall.

'The enchantment is in place, for sure,' he said, smiling his wicked smile.

Arthur did not understand until he stepped away down the passage. The door was concealed behind the image of a wall, and Branok slumbered within.

'How long will it hold?' said Arthur.

'Who can tell? It is not a science, but centuries, I think. It was thus for me,' said Merlin. 'Curse her.'

Arthur knew better than to push on this point. Merlin's activities between Camlann and taking on Branok as an apprentice were a mystery to him, and he knew it would remain so as long as the wizard had his way.

'Come then, we must find the others,' said Arthur.

He hurried back down through the White Tower and out once more into the courtyard.

The knights were standing clustered around something on the floor, some kneeling as though tending to a fallen man, some wiping blood from their blades and sheathing them.

The familiars had abandoned their human form and resembled ravens once more, strutting in the courtyard or standing, cawing, upon the White Tower or the surrounding walls.

Arthur's heart lurched to see his brothers assembled so, dreading to find out what evil their huddled bodies concealed. He rushed down the steps, sheathing his sabre as he ran and pushed between Gareth and Bedivere. Tristan knelt beside the fallen Geraint, who, Arthur saw, had suffered a gaping wound to his chest and another in his side. Geraint, the first of his knights to die since their awakening, stared up at the night sky with unseeing eyes.

They bore Geraint away to lay his body elsewhere, leaving Branok slumbering in the White Tower, and the ravens to bide their time as they might, haunting the Tower of London until their master walked free again.

Chapter Eighteen

London – 2019

Branok returned to his old haunt atop the White Tower and looked around at London's skyline, at its monstrous, mountainous buildings looming over the Thames, each illuminated from within like thin-skinned animals gathered at a waterhole with bellies full of fireflies. Daisy stood silently behind him.

'When William the Conqueror built the White Tower, it was a show of force, dominating the city below it. How it pales in comparison to these behemoths,' he said. 'You could stand on the south bank of the river and miss the fortress entirely.'

'Beautiful,' she said, and when Branok turned, he saw that she was referring to all that was new, reflected in the Thames to the south. He looked up at the Shard and nodded. *Progress.*

Branok turned and handed Daisy a folded newspaper. She took it and examined the front page. The headline read "LEADING THE CHARGE" over a photograph of the Home Secretary, Sir John Ransome, a middle-aged man in an ill-fitting suit, caught in a moment in which he was no doubt pontificating on whatever rhetoric would best appease or enrage the masses in order to lead to a vote for the new republic, Branok supposed. Daisy looked up at him, tilting her head to one side.

'Death or scandal, I leave it up to you, dear,' said Branok. 'Discredited or dead, it makes no difference to me.'

He looked at his watch then buried both hands deep into his pockets, shivering at the deep cold within his bones. Daisy took her raven form and, cawing, she took flight north over the city.

Branok closed his eyes and reached. The one he had selected was nearby.

David Bolton was still alive, but even his own family would have struggled to recognise him even a few short months after his family's demise. Once upon a time he had carefully shaved his face each morning and worn a suit five days in every seven. Now his beard and hair had grown out, he had mauled his fingernails, worrying them down until it was too painful to expose any more of the nailbed. He still wore the same clothes he had worn when he left his wife's deathbed months before. The Bolton family home remained intact and untouched some sixty miles away, preserved like a butterfly pinned in a glass case.

David refused to return to his house, as though crossing the threshold would allow in the reality that his family were dead. For now, it did not know. He would keep it so.

David had emptied his bank account and began to wander, ending up low on cash and without a place to stay on the streets of London. He fell into a bottle and there, damp from the vodka dregs, he dwelled still.

Branok had sensed him, sensed his pain, and reached out with his mind. Perhaps it was the warlock's meddling, or the trauma addling his mind, but David began to diminish in his grief.

Reality had become an abstract concept as he wandered the streets, where his perceptions, both real and imagined, mingled into a kaleidoscopic alcohol-hazed view of the world. One morning he passed a shop, closed for refurbishment, and knew in all certainty that a pile of snaking carpet offcuts on the doorstep were in fact discarded guts; entrails.

On another occasion, he was alone on a platform at King's Cross station until he was joined by a couple. They stood at the far end. The man was muscular, and the woman diminutive, her hair lank and shoulders stooped. They were both carrying shopping bags from an upmarket department store. David scrutinised them both and decided their appearance suggested that this shopping trip was something of a luxury as the quality of bags did not match the couple's clothes. Perhaps the man was annoyed at the expense. He was certainly angry about something. He stood with his arms folded and his feet pointing away from his partner. His wife, David corrected himself, noting her wedding ring.

The woman said something, reaching to touch her husband ever so lightly on the upper arm, but suddenly, violently, he wheeled away from her. His face contorted as he snarled in response. David's sense of alarm was lessened only by his drunken state as he watched from a nearby bench.

She protested, and the man raised his arm as though he was about to backhand her across the face, then thought better of it. Instead, he snatched those treasured shopping bags from her hands. He stood peacocking, his chest puffed out as he shouted then, ignoring her frantic cry, he threw the bags down onto the rail tracks and stormed away before the impact. When they struck the rails, David jumped at the sound of smashing porcelain. He saw the woman sink to her knees, sobbing, and, driven by an unexpected impulse as the man charged by him, David walked unsteadily up the platform towards the woman, feeling a desire to reach out to her in that forlorn moment.

But his eyes were drawn to the sight of broken, scattered shards of white plates upon the tracks. David stopped and stared, filled with that familiar, knowing disbelief that he was looking at broken bones, strewn down there where the rats would later pick at them.

He broke his gaze and staggered back towards the street in search of a new bottle.

David's makeshift home consisted of a few layers of cardboard underneath two sleeping bags, with yet more cardboard pulled across him.

He was just drifting off when someone grabbed his shoulder.

He spun away, raising his hands to guard his face and, lying on his side, he found himself staring at Branok, the warlock sitting on his haunches. The two men maintained eye contact in silence and a tension grew between them, though it was not unpleasant. David did not know Branok, as he had never met him before, and yet he felt he knew him intimately. He felt the same curious tickling pleasure in his spine that he had when his grandfather had taken time out of his day to sit and explain something which mattered only to him, yet was prepared to share with David. It made him feel…what?

Special, David decided. *Significant.*

'*You* are a brimming cup, my friend,' said Branok, as though confiding a true opinion about a close friend, certain and condescending.

'You are holding back the sea, looking back over your shoulder and pretending you are ashore,' said Branok, his will taking hold of his chosen man.

David did not understand, and yet he had to fight back tears as his heart heard some truth behind the words. He nodded.

'You must miss them terribly. Would you like me to release you? Let you return to them?' asked Branok, reaching out his hand. David took it without thinking.

'Come with me. Let's empty the cup and calm the ocean. You can be with your family, and I will make use of the shell you leave behind, this soon to be empty vessel.'

He smiled without humour, a cold smile, and yet there was eagerness behind his words.

Branok helped David to his feet and led him without a word, back towards the Tower, through the gates which opened before them without question, and up into the White Tower itself to Branok's chamber.

Branok closed the door and moved David across the room with a little force from the hand on his shoulder, and much more by intruding into the man's head.

Branok cast the circle around his victim, who now sat on the floor sipping at mulled wine from a cardboard cup they had bought from a street vendor on the route.

Quarters called and athame sheathed, Branok felt an immense energy building within his body. He walked slowly across the circle, feeling as though he was in a large hall, filled with an utterly silent audience who anticipated the precious moment when he began to finally speak. In a sense, it was true.

Branok sat before David, whose bleary eyes were fixed on some distant point.

'You'll be with them soon, friend,' said Branok, not knowing or caring whether it was true or not. His subject was pliable and all too ready to depart, and that was all that mattered to him.

The Ravenmaster began his incantations, and when a minute or an hour had passed, his stomach cramping and his hands shaking, Branok finally felt as though the rope he was hauling on gave way. It didn't snap or spring free, but gently eased itself loose. The soul of David Bolton left his body vacant.

Yet not for long, thought Branok. He knew he must

move swiftly now, and though he was near collapse, Branok began to call out for the one he sought, summoning him from beyond that great river none have crossed in life or, if they have, do not remember ever doing so.

Her task went against Daisy's instincts. The raven sometimes wondered who she had been in a past life, and what she had been like. She had been summoned from the crowded dead of Marston Moor, those Royalist troops who fell on that fateful day when Branok's first familiar had died, and so it seemed clear that she had been a soldier, but did that necessitate such a thirst for blood and death? Daisy thought not. She did not recognise the trait in her fellow ravens. Certainly they could be ruthless and single-minded, but Daisy did not detect any joy as they carried out their tasks.

She leaned back against the lamppost, aligning the metal with her spine where it touched between her shoulder blades. Her pale skin stood out against the loose-fitting black top, cut low to display her cleavage, and against the short skirt that only just disguised her modesty. The white skin of her legs was broken up by the interlacing lace of her stockings until they reached her calf-high stiletto boots. She positioned herself to best display her features, just as she had seen on billboards, and as she had seen women do when they wanted eyes on them.

A car pulled up alongside her. *The* car. The driver side window was drawn down by some mechanical contraption within the door, and Daisy could see Sir John Ransome looking out at her cautiously, but admiringly.

A few words exchanged. A deal proposed. A deal rejected. A few images captured.

Nathaniel watched the interaction through a long lens camera, snapping away until finally Daisy climbed into the back of the vehicle, and Sir John Ransome drove them away into the night.

Chapter Nineteen

'Our officers of cavalry have acquired a trick of galloping at everything. They never consider the situation, never think of manoeuvring before an enemy, and never keep back or provide a reserve.'
Sir Arthur Wellesley, Duke of Wellington

18th of June 1815 – Waterloo, The United Kingdom of the Netherlands

Around two o'clock in the afternoon, the Emperor Napoleon was winning the Battle of Waterloo.

Captain Arthur Grimwood, as he had taken to calling himself, waited to the north of a ridge with his company of British troopers as part of the Household Cavalry Brigade. It, along with the Union Cavalry Brigade, made up the Duke of Uxbridge's 2000 heavy cavalry. They were concealed by the ridge and, consequently, could not see the slaughter to the south, where the sunken main road was heavily contested by the infantry.

The artillery thundered, and the constant rattle of musket fire rose up and over the gathered soldiers with the smoke that drifted all across the battlefield.

'How long will we wait?' asked Percival for the fourth time.

'Quiet,' said Tristan, but he was grinning as he did so.

'Soon enough, I'm sure,' said Arthur, also grinning. Mounted on a fine dapple grey, he unsheathed his sabre and turned it over, inspecting both sides of the blade. He, like his knights, was dressed in the red coat of the British Army, and he wore a tall black hat.

The wait was interminable, yet despite their nervous anticipation, there was not a man amongst them who was not excited at the prospect of the coming charge.

This, thought Arthur, *is not so very different from the days of our youth. Less armour and the swords are far daintier, and yet never did I gather such numbers when I was king.*

And then it was on. The Duke of Uxbridge, somewhere at the front, gave the order. The trumpets blared out and a cry went up. The Household Brigade began to pour southwards over the ridge like boulders down a mountainside.

'With me!' called Arthur. 'For England!' and his knights echoed the cry. They spurred their horses and the charge of the British heavy cavalry began.

The ground shook beneath their horses' thundering hooves, and Arthur held his sword aloft, his face contorted into a grimace as he concentrated on the task ahead.

Before them the French cuirassiers were out of formation and vulnerable while they defended the infantry's flank. Arthur and the British rode through them.

Arthur hacked to his left and his right, smiting his foes with heavy blows from his sabre across their unprotected faces and throats, stabbing and thrusting, but always charging onwards. The cuirassiers gave way before the onslaught and were routed.

Now the Household Brigade advanced with all the momentum of their downhill charge straight at the 19th and 54th regiments of Aulard's brigade, smashing into the lines of the French infantry.

Arthur and his knights set to slaughtering the French soldiers, and carnage was everywhere about them, men crumpling in ragged messes as the gore ripped and drawn from their flesh by the British swords flicked this way and that, like paint flicked from a brush by a mad artist setting about his canvas. It was a hellish press of man and horse, of steel and flesh.

The Household Brigade destroyed their foe in a bloody onslaught.

Commanding officers called to their men, trying to get them under control, but the men's blood was up and all were frenzied. The orders went unheard or unheeded, and the British Household Cavalry continued their gallop to the east of the farm, La Haye Sainte.

Arthur, for his part, made no attempt to rein in his gallant company.

'Onward!' he urged his men. 'At them! On!'

Tristan rode to his left, and Percival to his right as they continued their gallop downhill until finally, their horses blown, shaking and panting, some dying beneath them, the Household Brigade reached the foot of the slope and there found the French infantry formed into squares, bristling with bayonets. They could advance no further.

Their charge was over, but not the battle.

Bors, Lamorak and Gaheris were with the Union Brigade as they charged through the British infantry and smashed into Bourgeois' brigade to begin their slaughter. The infantry destroyed or routed before them, both brigades were recovering from their charge when the French cuirassiers and lancers counter-charged. All descended into chaos. Major-General William Ponsonby, commander of the Union Brigade, was rallying his men when he was captured by a French sergeant, who killed him when his men attempted a rescue. Bors and Lamorak watched in dismay, unable to intervene, as that same sergeant cut down the would-be rescuers. At the loss of their leader, both knights exchanged a glance and rode off to find Arthur, abandoning their own regiment in so doing.

Not so very far away, just across the valley, Arthur thrust the tip of his sabre into the neck of a soldier then, looking about him, saw that Tristan was fighting alone amid a sea of lancers, cut off from his company and the rest of his brigade. Arthur watched in horror as the French closed about his knight, who fought on, but desperately, against the long lances of the enemy horsemen. Arthur called to his knights, but most were bogged down in their own battle.

Arthur spurred his horse on towards Tristan, but too many barred his way. He slashed and stabbed, parrying and kicking out to keep his foes at bay, but made slow progress.

He called out as he saw one of the lancers

spear Tristan's horse. The animal reared, and the last Arthur saw of Tristan was his knight attempting to swing a leg over the saddle so as to jump free before his mount collapsed atop him. The horse and rider fell to the ground, out of Arthur's view. He fought on all the harder, but again could make little progress forward to come to the aid of his knight.

Arthur drove his boot into a man's chest, pushing him so that he tripped and fell onto his back. Arthur looked up and saw Gaheris riding hard through the press of French infantry, not far from Tristan. Arthur called out to him, but his words were lost in the chaos of Waterloo. He saw Gaheris slash down to his left three times and turn the horse into the gap he had created. He closed in on the lancers and stabbed the first through the back. The man threw up his arms and collapsed sideways. His companions turned, and one stabbed out at Gaheris, but his knight reached out and grabbed the lance with his left hand and hauled the man from his saddle.

But the remaining lancer succeeded where his friend had failed. He drove his lance into Gaheris's mount. Gaheris leapt down and was lost from sight before the animal even reared.

'No,' said Arthur under his breath and redoubling his efforts to reach them. 'No.'

Finally he drew near and, to his relief, saw Tristan and Gaheris, both bloodied, fighting back-to-back against many enemies. Arthur rode down the soldiers before him and reared his mare so that her hooves struck out at the Frenchman beneath him. Arthur parried a blow from his right and wheeled his horse to close the distance between himself and the attacking lancer. Unable to pull back his weapon to strike again, the lancer fell without a chance to defend himself when Arthur drew back his sabre and cut the man's throat. The man toppled from the saddle, and Arthur called to his knights.

Tristan, who was bleeding heavily from his arm and leg, shouted something, but Gaheris propelled him towards the lancer's horse and, wearily, Tristan climbed into the saddle. Arthur reached down and hauled Gaheris up behind him. He felt his mare shudder with the extra weight, and for an alarming moment he thought she would collapse, but then she steadied. He spurred the horse on and, followed by Tristan, they retreated from the press in the valley to find the remainder of the British cavalry.

Arthur felt useful, felt vital, felt he could contribute once more. Wherever he rode upon that field, he rallied those around him who faltered. His voice, ever his power, more subtle but no less effective than that of Merlin or Branok, inspired many an act of courage that day, as it had throughout the Revolutionary and Napoleonic Wars. The cavalry suffered heavy losses as the battle progressed, officers and troops dying by the thousand, and Uxbridge could field fewer and fewer squadrons as the hours passed. Yet not one of Arthur's knights fell upon that field, in their element as they fought from the saddle with centuries of experience to hone their instincts and steady their nerve. They went merrily about their slaughter, confident that every dead Frenchman was a Frenchman that could no longer aid Napoleon in his attempt to win the day and, ultimately, invade Britain.

The remains of the Household Brigade drew together and repelled a combined attack by the French cavalry and infantry, and made themselves visible to the flagging infantry to embolden them when their numbers could not be put to better use. Once more Arthur's voice stirred the hearts of the troops, though they knew not the identity of this random cavalry captain who called out encouragement and praise. But when they heard his voice, their hearts were stirred and memories of both loved ones and of home filled their minds. They steadied, they held and they fought like warrior kings upon the field of Waterloo until finally the day was won.

The Duke of Wellington met Marshall Blucher at La Belle Alliance, the farm from where Napoleon had commanded his forces until he had been forced to retreat.

Six days later, Napoleon abdicated.

The threat from France had passed, and when the time came, Arthur and his knights returned to England once more.

Chapter Twenty

November 2019

Arthur dreamt he was doing battle with a great green serpent. He was unarmed and landing one ineffectual blow after another. The serpent lunged and wrapped itself around his torso, curling, tightening and squeezing so that Arthur began to choke and cough.

He awoke sweating and panicked, the sound of the smoke alarm raucous and loud enough to wake the whole house. It took him a moment to register the room was filled with churning grey smog, thick and unpleasant. Arthur thought to open the sash window and then realised that it was through it that the smog was pouring. He jumped to his feet and pushed the window fully up, leaning outside. The world was occluded by drifting banks of smog. Arthur spluttered and hacked as he closed the window.

'Arthur?' said a ragged voice from his doorway. When Arthur turned he saw Kay standing in a pair of trousers and a vest, hastily thrown on. He clasped a cloth over his nose and mouth.

'Close all the windows and put on all the extractors,' said

Arthur, feeling less than legendary as he stood coughing in his slippers, still half asleep and worrying about snakes.

'This can't be coincidence,' said Kay as they ate a large breakfast with the 24-hour news channel on in the background, telling tales of woe that had sprung up overnight. The smog was the least of it; tremors and sudden outbreaks of various illnesses, political scandals come to light, a controversial shooting, rioting and news of not one, but three assassinations of Russian officials that were being attributed to the British government. The newsreader, whom Arthur thought looked somewhat harried, suggested that such a catastrophic turn of events could be the precursor to war, that things had finally gone beyond the mounting sabre-rattling of recent months.

'Could Branok have really influenced so much?' asked Tristan.

'Last week I would have said that he was no match for Merlin,' said Arthur, 'but the blood-stained floorboards have proved me naïve.'

'Anything is possible,' said Bors. 'He's been brooding on this since they offed his last pet project.'

'But stirring things up with the Russians is new territory,' said Tristan. 'That goes way beyond the meddling of a wizard.'

Arthur laughed as he poured himself a whisky, standing at the kitchen table. His men looked at him, puzzled.

'Were it not for the meddling of a wizard, would we be

standing here today? They are more powerful than we imagine. We grow complacent. Merlin has largely been subtle in his practice, but Branok has never shown such restraint. Perhaps now we will find out just how much devastation one practitioner of the dark arts can cause,' said Arthur. He pulled out a chair and beckoned for the others to join him in sitting around the table. They passed the bottle round, each taking a swig of the whisky, some savouring the taste, and some pretending to do so while stifling a cough.

Arthur and the knights sat in silence as they drank, brooding on their situation, pondering how best to tackle the task ahead. Eventually though, the alcohol loosened the tension and their tongues. They fell into a lengthy debate which diverged into reminiscences and occasional arguments that generally ended with the majority of the men laughing.

'I'll ask a hard question,' said Arthur.

'As is your right,' proclaimed Tristan, a little louder than usual.

'I have never asked any of you to stand by me, or to while away the centuries in my service. In the beginning I thought loyalty was your duty and my right, but for many years now, I have wondered why you all stay with me in this new world where our role is so diminished. I am no king. You are not knights. Why do you spend your lives in endless service beyond any expectation of man?' said Arthur, ending by once more lifting his glass to his lips.

'I am still a knight of your court, as I will ever be,' said Tristan.

'You're a god-damned scallywag, is what you are!' said Bors with a wave of his hand. The others chuckled, and Arthur smiled, but Tristan remained grim-faced until the noise died down, and the more empathic among them scrutinised him, trying to gauge his reaction.

'The oaths I made do not end in death or get wiped away by new life,' said Tristan. 'I followed you when I was young, when this land was young, and I pledged my sword to you, forever. I mean to honour my commitments, as is our way.' He reached for the bottle and drank deep. 'I cannot, however, speak for the rest of the company.'

Murmurs of assent burbled around the table like quiet waters over stones, yet Arthur was not content.

'What would you say if I were to release you?' he asked, his eyes fixed on a knot in the wooden surface of the oak table.

Tristan frowned, sitting back in his chair as though considering an insult thrown by a stranger in a tavern.

'As a fantasy or a possibility?' asked Kay. His tone was artificially light, and in this Arthur perceived a hidden truth. The old clock on the wall ticked the seconds away.

'If you were not constrained in answering,' said Arthur. 'If you could speak from the heart.'

Tristan folded his arms across his chest.

Arthur looked around the table at his knights, searching for answers, and in their faces he found them. He saw the wives and children they never had, he saw the dreams of peace and even rest. And in some he saw the fierce desire to be out in the world at large, engaging in its forward motion, rather than bobbing on the river surface or being anchored to the past.

Kay was about to speak, but Arthur held up his hand.

'It is enough that you have answered for yourselves, I need not hear it,' he said. 'Let fate play out without herald.'

He took the bottle from Bors and screwed on the lid. He held it up before him and rotated it in his hand, watching the caramel-coloured spirit swirl around the bottom.

'I do not know if we can defeat him,' said Arthur at last, 'and even if we can, I think not all of us will survive. Another hard question. Are you prepared to make that sacrifice? No,' said Arthur. 'Do not answer with your first instincts, but with heart's truth. We are not the heroes of old, warriors of legend that exist in the storybooks, embellished by each new author. We are not even that ragged band which became war leaders when the Romans fled these shores. There is no nation to forge, and in truth, I have lost all notion of countries and nations. We are here, in this land, *of* this land, and in truth, it is as unified as it will ever be. What little can we do, but the ordinary good that can be done by any with wealth and influence. This reckoning with Branok will be the last chapter in the myths of this land, the last battle which only we can fight, for he is one of us, one of Merlin's adopted few. None will know we fought this battle, whether we lived or died in it, and we will have no thanks either way. If we fail? Well, we have seen what his contagion has done before in the days when his powers were but fledgling and yet to take full flight. Many will die until his ends are achieved.'

'His ends will never be fully achieved. This land, this England, it is an ever-changing thing,' said Kay, quietly. 'All loyalties to anything but one's neighbour are fleeting by necessity. Time and time again, the people will attempt to throw down the last vestiges of old empire and even more ancient kingdoms in favour of some new republic. It is inevitable, and Branok will fight them down the ages. We cannot let it stand.'

'Hear, hear,' said Tristan, and he took the bottle from Arthur once more to drink his fill.

'To this last battle, and an end to the legend,' said Tristan, 'if not to loyalty.'

'A final battle,' nodded Arthur. 'And when it is done, I will set you all free to go where you wish. You have all served and suffered long enough. No king could ask more of his knights than I have of you, and no knight could serve more faithfully than have those who are gathered here.'

The bottle passed around the circle once more in silence.

By mid-afternoon Arthur had sobered once more, and the sound of a key turning in the front door lock signalled that the company were soon to be full assembled. Sure enough, Merlin and his escort paraded into the hall, all of them laden with bags and disguised swords, save for Merlin who made straight for the nearest armchair. Arthur greeted his knights and followed the old man into the sitting-room on the first floor of the townhouse.

'No sign, I take it,' said Arthur.

Merlin shook his head.

'I always suspected he would be here, at the heart of government and the seat of power,' said Merlin, 'and I imagine I am not alone in that.'

'No, not alone,' said Arthur, 'but we had to be sure. Things are moving apace now, Merlin. Branok is exerting all of his influence. We must move against him. Tonight.'

The old man leaned forward in the armchair, elbows on his knees, his hands draped over one another. He sighed and looked up to meet Arthur's gaze.

'The White Tower?' said Arthur.

'I imagine so,' said the wizard. 'He is near. I can feel his breath on my neck.'

Merlin shuddered.

'Take your rest. We strike on the stroke of four, before the dawn,' said Arthur. 'We all go.'

While Merlin slept, each of Arthur's knights prepared his arms, his mind and his soul as seemed fit to him. Many of them took the opportunity to sleep, rest or pray before the allotted time, which came all too soon. It was odd, thought Arthur, to realise one may have seen one's last sunset. He woke those who were sleeping one by one, leaving Merlin till the very last minute, knowing that it would take all of the wizard's strength to contest Branok's power.

When they were all assembled in the hall, each of them armed with a sword, amongst other weapons, except for Merlin who carried only his staff, Arthur stood before them.

'Tonight we put an end to Branok and his familiars,' said Merlin.

'And we all know where we will find them,' said Arthur as he pulled on his black woollen coat. He withdrew his Colt from his shoulder holster, snapped it open and confirmed it was fully loaded.

'At them, sir?' said Tristan, grinning.

'At them,' said Arthur. 'Through them if we must.'

Chapter Twenty-One

30th of June 1916 –The First World War

Arthur could tune out the crackling rifle fire and distant artillery explosions, but his guilt prevented him from immersing himself in his book, the text barely visible by the meagre light afforded by his Orilux torch and a cluster of candles, rammed into empty glass bottles. Arthur sighed, closed the book, its pages crinkled from days of wetting and drying out, some spotted with black mould.

He sat stooped in a rickety chair, the back of his hair tickling against the low ceiling of the dugout. His was a narrow space in which he was hemmed in by a wooden post, supporting the ceiling, and the planks covering the walls. And yet even in such a sparse environment, he knew that his men had it far worse in their makeshift shelters or, worse, funk holes, dug into the walls of the trench itself.

On the other side of the subterranean

dwelling, Lieutenant Daniel Phillips seemed to be having a little more success in relaxing. He sipped at his brandy as he made his way through a pile of old letters from his wife.

Arthur stood, still stooping, and began to pull on his trench coat in order to check in with the men. He drew his recently acquired Colt revolver from its holster, checking it was loaded out of habit and then put it away. Before he reached the door, there was a knock and Phillips called for whoever it was to enter.

A young man of about eighteen entered and saluted.

'Post, sir,' said the boy to Arthur, presumably as he was standing.

'I suppose I hope in vain that our provision box has come from London?' he replied.

'Sir, afraid so, sir,' said the boy. He drew four letters from his bag.

'Two for Lieutenant Daniel Phillips, one for Lieutenant Simon Marwood and one for Captain Arthur Grimwood.'

Arthur took the letters and dismissed the soldier. He handed Phillips his letters, made his way to the rear of the dugout to where Marwood was sleeping in one of three wire beds screened off by a partition wall. He placed the letter on the sleeping man's chest, then set off back to his chair to read his own post, doubtless from someone at the company, his solicitor or his accountant. The world was at war, no doubt, but business went on back in Blighty.

Arthur heard a strangled moan from the common area before he'd rounded the partition wall. The top of his spine tickled and his throat constricted, knowing instinctively what was coming.

He paused then continued walking, readying himself.

Phillips was still seated, a torn envelope on the wooden duckboards beside his chair and the single page of the letter held in a trembling hand.

Arthur bent to pick up the envelope and placed a comforting hand on the younger man's shoulder. Phillips flinched at the touch, but continued staring at the page even when Arthur plucked it from his shaking fingers.

It was as he had suspected.

Phillips's father-in-law informed him, with regret, that his young wife had died three days after giving birth to their daughter. He conveyed his own grief and his sadness that Phillips was forced to open two such letters in such a short space of time.

Arthur was confused momentarily and then, realising, his eyes settled on the second unopened letter waiting on the table beside him.

The baby, thought Arthur.

"GAS! GAS! GAS!" someone shouted from above. Phillips jumped to his feet automatically as the warning rattles began to sound. Despite Arthur's concern, the lieutenant found his makeshift respirator, a urine soaked sock, as though he were working on automatic. Arthur secured his own as he ran to wake Marwood. When he returned, Phillips had secured the gas-curtain in place over the doorway.

1st of July 1916 – The First Day of the Battle of the Somme – The First World War
0728hrs.

Arthur's company were assembled with bayonets fixed, leaning up against the wall of the trench when the mines exploded, ripping apart German defences and tearing great craters in no-man's-land.

'Bloody hell, sir,' said Tristan as the roar of the explosions thundered on.

'Easy now, Sergeant,' replied Arthur. He turned to address his gathered men, among them not only the working-class men of England, but some of his knights, Gawain, Galahad, Percival, Gareth, Bors, Kay, Dagonet, Lamorak and Gaheris. The rest were spread out along the western front.

'Men, all I ask is...' but suddenly whistles began to blow, and he too placed a whistle to his lips and blew.

It begins, he thought as he clambered up the ladder, closely followed by his knights, his officers and his men.

'Onward!' roared Arthur, drawing his sword and holding it aloft as he charged through the smoke towards the German frontline, the battlefield of no-man's-land masked by drifting banks of smoke. Cordite and blood-iron scented the air.

This was it, thought Arthur, this was what he could contribute in this modern age. King Arthur would lead his fellow countrymen into glorious battle at their time of need.

Perhaps they were just being brought into action, startled by the sudden ferocity of the attack or perhaps Arthur was just hearing them for the first time, the German machine-guns fired as his company rushed on, clambering over barbed wire, their boots sinking in patches of quagmire between the fallen soldiers, whose bare skulls grinned up from the mud. The air filled with zipping bullets, explosions and screams, artillery thundering on and on. Arthur checked to either side of him and found Galahad and Lamorak running beside him.

The smoke grew thicker. Had seconds or minutes passed? Arthur could not tell. And yet still no enemy to fight. He lowered his sword, concentrating on the ground before him. Then Galahad cried out, gurgling as bullets stitched across his chest and throat. He fell back dead and Lamorak fell beside him. Arthur felt the weight of their loss, of their centuries of kinship as though he had been shot in the head. He staggered, the hem of his coat dipping into the mud, and then, seeing his company overtake him, he rushed after them, leaving his knights to die alone.

Arthur screamed as he ran, screamed for his men to have courage and to keep on. He screamed the same orders over and over, as he passed the broken remains of Lieutenant Daniel Phillips, who had gone to meet his wife and daughter, and of Lieutenant Marwood, though he did not know it for the man's head was gone. Arthur charged onward, thinking that if he could just reach the enemy, he would make an account of himself to shame even the legends of his past.

A bullet smashed through his left calf and Arthur pitched forward into the mire. He crawled forward and looked ahead of him but there was nothing to see but smoke and flashes of explosions through it. All around him his company groaned and cried out and fell silent.

Arthur tried to stand but his leg was shattered. Live fire whistled all around him, and he was forced to throw himself on his face.

The pain became too much and, as Arthur went into shock, his knights began to fall, just like so many men, all along the western front.

Blinding light. Where was he?

Arthur had begun to think the worst when he saw a shaded electric lightbulb hanging above him and felt a relatively soft mattress beneath him.

'That,' said a familiar voice, 'is a Blighty.'

Arthur blinked, letting his eyes adjust and found Tristan standing above him in a clean uniform, leaning on a stick and pointing at Arthur's leg.

'Home for you,' said Tristan, smiling a weak, cold smile.

'Hospital?' asked Arthur, and Tristan nodded.

Arthur felt hungover, his head swimming. He didn't know who they had lost and yet he felt the losses without needing to be told. Did it matter who? He knew exactly what had befallen his company, and surely what had befallen all of his brothers who had come to fight in the trenches.

He draped his forearm across his eyes as he began to sob.

Tristan sat on a chair beside Arthur's bed, but he said nothing.

Finally Arthur asked for the butcher's bill, but it took Tristan quite a while to begin answering.

'We only have estimates, sir, but the numbers are grievously high,' Tristan admitted.

'How many?' said Arthur again.

'Impossible to say, sir. You were pulled out by a chap called Goody. He'll get a medal, like as not, but there are still plenty of the men unaccounted for as of yet. Still between the lines.'

'Tristan,' said Arthur, gripping his knight's wrist.

'If you're going to press me, sir, I'd say twenty to forty per cent casualty rate, including the injured, but that's no more than a guess, sir,' said Tristan, taking Arthur's hand in his own.

Arthur stared up at the ceiling, unable to comprehend.

'Forty per cent,' he whispered.

'A rough estimate,' said Tristan.

'This is on my head,' said Arthur through tears. 'I had no business leading men in battle. I'm a relic and should have consigned myself to the past.'

'If that's true, it's true of most of the commanders,' said Tristan. 'Our losses are not so different from anyone else's.'

Arthur said nothing, attempting to regain his composure.

'This is not war as I understand it,' he said.

Tristan held his hand a little firmer.

'I never even saw their faces,' said Arthur.

'You should be glad of that,' said Tristan, his voice low. 'I saw them. I reached them.'

Arthur sought to meet his knight's gaze, but Tristan lowered his eyes.

'What of our brothers?' said Arthur.

'Galahad, Gaheris and Lamorak are gone from our company. I have heard no word from the rest as of yet,' said Tristan, 'but I think we should prepare ourselves.'

Arthur winced as the pain in his leg flared.

And as the Battle of the Somme raged on, Arthur accepted sedation and slept.

Chapter Twenty-Two

London – November 2019

As Arthur's foot stepped down and touched the pavement, the ground shook, and he fell back against the rail. He clung on while the tremor subsided, watching as windows shattered in the old building opposite. Glass shards fell onto the street and tinkled on the concrete below.

Arthur held his scarf over his mouth against the foul fumes that swirled about him under the streetlights and, accompanied by the racket of a thousand car and burglar alarms sounding, he advanced down the street. The doors of the neighbouring houses opened up and people spilled into the night, as people are inclined to do when faced with an unexpected act of nature, or at least, something approximating an unexpected act of nature. They looked about, alarmed, and went back inside, those who did not seek their cars in order to start the journey to escape the capital.

The streetlights went out, as did the lights in the buildings all around. A raven's call could be heard above, but its flight went unseen in the meagre light afforded by the moon and stars.

'Come on,' said Arthur without turning back. 'He's calling to us.'

He limped onwards, and Merlin fell in beside him.

Any thoughts of taking a cab or driving disappeared as a mob swarmed across the junction at the end of the street. Arthur saw a lit petrol bomb career in a high arc across the sky and explode against a police car as it screeched to a halt, its sirens blaring and blue lights aglow.

Arthur saw his knights line up beside him in his peripheral vision. Together, in a line, they paced towards the mob. They were an unruly lot, working as a horde rather than a unified force. Arthur doubted they wanted anything more than to bask in the chaos.

They had been seen and several individuals wielding iron bars and baseball bats, their faces covered in ski masks, charged towards them, peacocking, arms wide, necks exposed, and 'Come and get me', written all over them in invisible ink.

They drew closer, shouting and hurling eggs, which fell short, splattering the road with yolk and white.

Merlin held up his staff and the weapons fell from their hands as their jaws fell slack.

'Be gone,' he growled, and, drearily, as though sleep-walking, the men turned about and slowly walked back in the direction they had come.

Arthur, Merlin and company pressed on through a city clogged with rioting youths, who rampaged through the smog, doing battle with the riot police. Arthur saw broken windows everywhere and cars on fire. The ground shook beneath their feet as they walked.

'Look at that,' said Bors as they rounded a corner just in time to see a gaggle of protestors, lit by the fires, smash into the police lines. They crunched against the shields as bricks and petrol bombs flew overhead. The officers held their ground and their batons flew, but there were too few of them.

'That,' said Bors, 'Is what you get if you vote Tory!'

It took Arthur's company nearly two hours to cross the city, and it was nigh on three in the morning when they finally stood before the Tower of London.

'Are you all ready?' said Arthur.

'Aye,' said Tristan, who spoke for all of the men without need for conversation.

'Branok's chambers are high in the White Tower itself,' said Merlin.

'We go in as we did before,' said Arthur. 'If the ravens lie between us and the Ravenmaster, all of you must take them on while Merlin and I go on to deal with Branok.'

'Won't he be expecting that?' said Tristan. 'He knows full well we are coming, Arthur. He won't be as naïve as to sit waiting for us.'

'What other choice do we have?' said Arthur.

'He's correct, boy,' said Merlin. 'Branok may well match us this time, where before we caught him off guard.'

'Nevertheless,' said Arthur. 'We proceed as I have said, unless any man amongst you has another suggestion.'

Tristan made no further protest, murmuring, 'so be it' as he walked towards the Tower.

They climbed over the barriers by the ticket booths and advanced on the gatehouse. Whenever they encountered anyone, Merlin used his arts to beguile them and so the company passed on through until finally they were inside the Tower itself.

The sight before them struck all still and quiet.

The floor between them and the steps to the White Tower were black. A carpet of thousands of ravens stood before them, strutting about, fighting, and flying here and there, indistinguishable from one another. Thousands of beady black eyes turned to look at Arthur, Merlin and the knights. One by one, the knights drew their broadswords, and Arthur, last of all, drew the very same cavalry sabre that he had wielded at Waterloo.

'What now?' asked Kay, and Arthur made no answer, merely standing surveying the scene, looking for some sign that might betray one of the familiars.

The ground rumbled beneath them, and Arthur looked up as a crack opened in the west wall of the White Tower.

'Onward,' he muttered. 'There is no other choice.'

With that he stalked forward, holding up his sabre, picking his way between the birds. The others rushed to join him far less delicately, and the birds called out, flapping up from under their feet.

Arthur led the company across the courtyard, cautious

that at any time the familiars could strike. And yet, he thought, would they? They had plenty of opportunities to assault Arthur or his people in the days since the attack on his home. Had a raven not watched his progress when he arrived in London? What was Branok planning?

Arthur had no idea.

He walked onward, his blood whooshing in his ears.

Any second now, the attack would come. Any second.

Arthur could hear Tristan and Gareth's rapid breathing beside him and knew they too were feeling as though they were looking up at the sword of Damocles.

But the attack never came. Arthur and Merlin ran up the steps to the White Tower as the knights turned to face the ravens and guard the rear. As the two men walked towards the doors, they swung open, revealing the dimly lit interior of the White Tower, so different from the last time Arthur had entered. Artefacts stood around the rooms, which were now laid out to display the arms and armour of the kings and queens of Britain.

Not a sound. No movement.

Arthur turned to ask Merlin if he felt able to go on, but he saw a grim expression on the wizard's face and perceived a dark fire within his old mentor, who stood straighter than his aged spine would normally allow.

'Quickly,' said Merlin and disappeared into the White Tower. Arthur paused only to look back at his knights for a second then followed on, wondering if he would ever step out into the starlight again.

Across the wooden floors, up steps and through narrow corridors, Merlin and Arthur made their progress through the Tower. Each felt unseen eyes upon them as they stalked the fortress where so many had died over the centuries, this bastion of strength, symbol of enduring power.

On and on they went, still meeting no opposition. Arthur strained to hear if battle had been joined in the yard outside, but all was silent save for the sounds of their feet and the noise of their laboured breathing. Arthur limped, his leg crying out, and every so often he would steady Merlin, who no longer had an arm to thrust out to break any fall. Battered and wounded, the mentor and the pupil, the wizard and the king climbed ever higher, until, finally, they came to the spot.

Arthur laid his hand upon the stone wall and drew it back sharply as it seemed to ripple away from him.

Why was he in this place? And what was the significance of the wall? Merlin's seal may have been broken, but the enchantment he had laid upon the stone was no less potent.

Arthur's puzzled face looked to Merlin for answers. The wizard nodded towards the wall.

'Branok lies beyond. I can feel him,' he whispered, and Arthur remembered their quest, as one might remember the plot of a dream for seconds after waking.

Merlin muttered, his brow furrowing in annoyance, then gestured with his fingers. Suddenly the effect wore off, and Arthur was no longer deceived. He knew his purpose and before him, he saw a door where previously there had only been stone.

'Branok lies beyond,' he repeated to himself. Merlin nodded.

'Ready, boy?'

Arthur nodded.

'Ready,' he whispered.

Merlin reached for the handle, and, in a flash of movement which belied his age, he thrust the door inward.

Arthur burst through the open door into the candlelit cell, closely followed by Merlin. The wizard's remaining hand held out his staff, and Arthur could feel the power emanating from it, the exertion of will.

David Bolton stood in the centre of a salt circle with his back to the door. He was looking down at what Arthur mistook for a bundle of rags, but quickly realised was a man.

'Branok,' Merlin exclaimed, putting a name to the figure on the floor, and sure enough, Arthur recognised the warlock. But he was much changed. Branok's short black hair was a shocking white, his beard grown out and fully silver. His skin hung like melting beeswax and his eyes were rheumy. The air reeked. His whole body lurched with every stolen breath as it lay within the centre of the circle.

Arthur raised his sabre, pointing the tip between David Bolton's shoulder blades. He drew the Colt from his left pocket.

'Who are you?'

When the man turned, Arthur saw he was grinning and Excalibur hung at his hip. He did not recognise David

Bolton's face, but heard Merlin gasp and step back.

'Run, boy,' said the wizard. 'Run if ever you trusted me.'

Arthur levelled the Colt so he was aiming at the man's heart.

'Who are you?' he demanded, but the man drew Excalibur and in that instant, recognising the hungry, lusting look in the man's otherwise unfamiliar face, at last, Arthur realised just who he was facing.

'Mordred,' he said, and moved to parry as his son used Excalibur to slash at his father's side.

It cleaved through the sabre like it wasn't there at all. Arthur staggered forwards with his own momentum, exposed. Merlin sprang forward to aid him.

Mordred, wearing David Bolton's empty body like a costume, wheeled, and as he did so, he brought up the blade, slashing sideways.

And he struck Merlin's head from his shoulders.

Chapter Twenty-Three

Sussex, England
1940 – The Second World War

'Do me proud,' said Arthur as he stirred the pot of stew he had been working on for an hour in his new house, nestled within its walled estate, deep in the woods.

Tristan nodded.

'Will do, sir,' he smiled, and Arthur detected pity in the gesture, but he said nothing as guilt washed over him. Tristan, dressed in his khaki Home Guard uniform, looked out into the hall, where the others were gathering, ready to leave.

'Keep safe tonight, sir,' said Tristan, raising his eyebrows in expectation of reassurance, and Arthur obliged.

'I will, I will,' said Arthur. 'I'll leave stew in the pot for when you chaps get back.'

'You don't have to, sir,' said Percival, dressed identically to Tristan, as he stepped into the room.

'I want to,' said Arthur. 'Get going or you'll miss parade and let me down.'

Arthur and his knights did not age, and they had looked in their thirties when they fought at the Somme. After the war they had maintained the same identities, and so, when war was declared on Germany in 1939, some twenty-one years after Armistice Day, they were too old to be conscripted. Locally, there was talk about their youthful looks, but none could deny their war records, and so, with a little subtlety and making a great show of keeping in shape, Arthur's knights avoided most of the negative comments one could expect if one had avoided the draft.

However, none of them were happy about it, and when the Local Defence Volunteers were initiated in 1940, later becoming the Home Guard, Tristan went to Arthur and gained permission for the brothers to sign up, which all of them did. They, Tristan said, might not be able to go abroad to fight, but they would damn well defend England if it came to it.

An organisation made up of those too old, too young or too ill for conscription, the Home Guard were eventually tasked with delaying the advance of German invading forces until the regular army could regroup. But it was not long before Tristan and the knights wearied of parading with such folk, well-intentioned and noble as they might be. They were still in their prime, warriors beyond comparison, returned from the grave to defend Britain, and yet they lined up in their own clothes with only armbands to mark them out until finally uniforms were issued, beside the inexperienced, the too-experienced and the infirm.

Tristan grew frustrated, but the Home Guard had hidden depths unknown to the public at large. A British resistance effort had been planned and would now be catered for, and the Home Guard was scouted for the best and the brightest. Tristan and the knights shone out beyond all others.

Almost nobody knew of the Auxiliary Units, not even their families. They were secret units who paraded with the Home Guard, but who had their own mission and mandate; they were known amongst themselves as the Scallywaggers.

Tristan and the other knights attended secret training sessions at Coleshill House in Wiltshire, where they learned to 'scallywag', which was their term for unarmed combat, assassinations, guerrilla warfare, demolition and sabotage. Upon returning home, Tristan led an operational patrol consisting of Agravain,

Kay, Lucan, Gareth, Gawain, Bors and Dagonet while the others gave service elsewhere in the country in various forms.

Once the meeting of the Home Guard was over, the Scallywags melted into the night, disappearing down country lanes and into the woods.

Tristan moved in the cover of the trees at the rear of the group, watching to ensure that they had not been followed.

Before half an hour had passed, they found a gap in the ridge of the hills, the beginning of a medieval track that villagers had used to drive their herds to the common grazing lands atop the hill before the trees had been planted in later centuries. Using the track, the Scallywags could move beneath the level of the ground and out of line of sight. Before long they reached a point that would have drawn no attention to anyone unaware of the secret it held. Here the Royal Engineers had delved an entrance into the unit's operation base. The door, hinged at the top, was disguised with turf and undergrowth. Bors hauled it open, and the Scallywags disappeared underground.

As was their routine, they scouted out the bunker, checking that nothing had been disturbed, that their MKIIS silenced Sten guns, pistols, silencers, ammunition and munitions were all accounted for and secure. Tristan personally checked the food stores while Dagonet moved down the tunnel leading to the emergency exit.

From here they would launch their campaign against the Nazis, should they successfully invade England, with orders to commit suicide or kill one another, rather than allow any of their number to be captured.

The Scallywags set about maintaining their base and, when an hour had passed, they left it secure and headed home to feast on steaming bowls of stew and hot buttered toast.

Arthur wandered the darkened streets of his town. He was clad in a dark blue boilersuit with a satchel containing his gas mask slung across his chest. He wore both a steel helmet marked with a white 'W' and a white band with ARP printed on it over his upper arm. Arthur's leg had never fully healed from the injury sustained at the Somme, and he usually walked with a cane. While fulfilling his duties as an air raid warden, however, he walked with the aid of a three-metre-long steel ceiling pike with a hook on the end, for use in searching bombed-out buildings. Laden also with a pump and hose, for fighting fires, and a wooden rattle for sounding a gas attack, Arthur walked alone, thinking of his knights, both at home and those who had managed to get abroad. He pondered his own role, and considered whether he could take a combatant role of some kind. But each time he entertained a possibility, his chest seemed to tighten, and he thought that he might pass out. Sweat beaded on his forehead, and he heard once more the explosions and screams, saw Gaheris crashing to the ground.

All was calm and quiet as Arthur crossed the deserted high street, checking that the blackout was entirely in place, looking for any light emitting from the swathed windows of houses and businesses.

As he passed the graveyard, a torch beam burst from between the graves, blinding him.

'Put that light out!' Arthur shouted, recoiling as he shaded his eyes with his hand. 'Out, now!'

Instead the torch-wielder lowered the beam to illuminate a small rectangular gravestone; a familiar gravestone, well-tended, devoid of creepers, with a single pebble resting atop it.

Arthur quickened his pace and entered the graveyard through a small kissing-gate then made his way along the various paths towards the gravestone and whoever was standing over it. Arthur had his suspicions.

Sure enough, Merlin stood looking down at the grave, one hand thrust into the pocket of his long green army trench coat and a torch in the other. His long hair was tied back in a ponytail which hung down at the waist.

'Good evening, boy,' he said, not looking up from the stone.

'Merlin,' Arthur replied as he came to stand beside the old wizard. He looked down at Gaheris's gravestone.

Corporal Simon Humphrey - 1886 – 1916 -
Killed in Action

'Corporal,' said Merlin. 'A knight of King Arthur, a lowly corporal.'

'There's nothing lowly about being a corporal, Merlin,' Arthur snapped.

'Years since we have seen one another and that is the tone you take with me?' said Merlin, turning to face him.

'When you disrespect the fallen, absolutely,' said Arthur.

Neither man said anything further for a time. Arthur eventually pointed at a group of graves a little further in.

'Galahad and Lamorak are lying side-by-side, I see,' said Merlin.

'These graves are empty. They were laid to

rest in Belgium,' said Arthur.

'I see. A memorial?' asked Merlin, and Arthur nodded.

They stood silently for a while, Arthur out of respect for his fallen knights. Merlin? Who could tell?

'What brings you back after so long?' asked Arthur. 'Is all forgiven?'

'It is not a matter of forgiveness, Arthur. You have a duty to fulfil, and I will not stand by your side while you wilfully shirk it.'

'I have served this country as best I can since my return,' said Arthur. 'I have fought in more wars than anyone alive.'

'Oh? Is that correct?' Merlin rapped his knuckles on Arthur's steel helmet. 'Do you fight now? No. And aren't your knights off at war? They appear to have fought in more wars than you, boy.'

'I would be with them if it wasn't for my leg,' said Arthur.

'Regrettable incident,' said Merlin, who jumped as Arthur let out a laugh at the absurd reductive summary of the first day of the Somme.

'I amuse you, boy?' said Merlin, but Arthur shook his head in silence.

'How bad is it?' asked Merlin, softer.

'Bad enough that I need a cane and failed the medical,' said Arthur.

Merlin nodded and took hold of Arthur by his right wrist so that he looked up and into the wizard's eyes.

'Not the leg,' said Merlin. 'How bad is it?'

Arthur could feel Merlin poking around in his mind, saw the old man's eyes widening and his face twitch. Arthur wrenched his arm free of his mentor's grasp, but the wizard stepped in and took him in an embrace, there, in the dark in the midst of the dead and the memory of the fallen.

1940 – World War Two - London

London might have been as dark as its smaller counterparts, but its skies were far busier, as the Luftwaffe made their night-time bombing runs which, during the course of the Blitz, practically eradicated the East End of London.

While Branok slept, unable to intervene to protect the bloodline, a bomb first fell in the grounds of Buckingham Palace on the 8th of September 1940. The following day, another landed, causing some damage to the building itself. Yet it was not until the morning of the 13th of September that a single German bomber managed to drop five bombs on to the palace while the 14th monarch to have reigned since

Merlin incapacitated Branok, King George VI, and his queen, Elizabeth, were in residence taking tea. They escaped unscathed, though one man died in the blast.

The palace would be bombed on many more occasions, and yet the bloodline endured, even as the ravens wandered the Tower of London, unable to intervene.

The Royal Family remained in London, showing solidarity with their people, who never loved them more than they did by the end of that war. And all while Branok slept.

Chapter Twenty-Four

The Tower of London – November 2019

Arthur fell to his knees as his stomach convulsed. He vomited over David Bolton's laces as Merlin's body slumped to the floor beside him. The wizard's head rolled across the floorboards. Arthur's stomach voided again, and, too bereft to do anything else, he rolled onto his back and shuffled back towards the door. As Mordred sheathed Excalibur, Arthur swapped the Colt into his right hand and once more levelled it at David Bolton's chest with a shaking hand.

'The King is dead. Long live the King,' said Branok. He took up Merlin's staff and used it as an aid to stand.

'I warned you,' said Branok, who now looked older than Merlin himself. Arthur kept his eyes on Mordred, unable to fully comprehend in that dreadful moment.

'I told you not to come,' said Branok, as though he were a child justifying some indiscretion to his parents. 'I took precautions.' Still Arthur did not look at him.

'We are wasting time,' said Mordred.

'Do not move,' said Branok. 'He holds a weapon.'

David Bolton's eyes had seen many a firearm, on

television and in museums, at least, but Mordred frowned and looked at the Colt, unable to see *how* it could be so.

Arthur thumbed back the hammer and the chamber rotated.

'Father?' said Mordred.

'You are an ill-begotten bastard, born of incest,' said Arthur as he tried to steady his shaking hand. He was far from confident he could make the shot even at such close quarters. And could he even bring himself to pull the trigger?

Mordred smiled.

'An ancient lie to discredit your sister. Aunt Morgana is long dead, Father, and it does not behove you to speak ill of those who cannot defend themselves.'

He looked at Branok.

'Unless she is attending, and I am caught unawares?'

'She is not,' said Branok, who looked as though he had aged fifty years in an evening from the effort of summoning and binding Mordred's soul to David Bolton's body.

Arthur reached up with his left hand and steadied the revolver.

'Why?' he asked Branok, although he knew full well.

'He defeated you once, and he will again, without a doubt now that Merlin is gone,' said Branok as he stooped. He took a handful of Merlin's hair and lifted the head up, cradling it in his arms. He stepped over the wizard's sprawled legs and made for the door. As he walked between Arthur and Mordred, Branok gestured with his left hand and Arthur, ensnared momentarily, lowered the Colt.

'Good lad, Arthur,' said Branok as he disappeared into

the hall. Mordred stepped in quickly and, curious, pulled the revolver from his father's trembling hands. He turned it over in his hands and pointed it at Arthur, looping his finger around the trigger.

'You learn fast,' said Arthur.

Mordred pulled the trigger.

The bullet slammed into the stone wall beside Arthur's head. The recoil took Mordred entirely by surprise, and Arthur dived forward, slamming his shoulder into his son's legs, squeezing them together. Mordred toppled over backwards onto the stone floor amid Branok's salt circle, trapping Arthur's right arm beneath him. Arthur's face pressed against Excalibur's hilt for a moment and then he hauled his arm free as Mordred recovered and began to lower the revolver to take aim. Arthur threw himself onto Mordred's torso, pushing the gun aside. Mordred punched him in the top of the head with staggering force, then bucked to shift his father onto the floor.

Branok emerged into the night and stood atop the steps up to the White Tower.

'Behold,' he said, and the knights' heads snapped round at the sound of his voice. They stared in horror as Branok held up Merlin's severed head for all to see.

'Get him,' roared Bors and 'Take him,' shouted Tristan as they burst up the steps towards him.

Branok smiled and held up Merlin's staff. The two men stood in place and lowered their blades.

The warlock cast Merlin's head between them and it bounced down the last few steps, coming to rest at the feet of the remaining knights.

Branok clicked his fingers, and his familiars took their human forms. They moved silently through the ravens at their feet towards the assembled knights, menacing and relentless.

'Where is Arthur?' called Kay.

'He lies within,' said Branok. 'Will you fight us or save him?' But he thought from the rage in Tristan's eyes, the answer might be both and that discretion might be the better part of valour on this occasion. Still holding up the staff, he pushed between the two men and carried on down the steps, holding the knights in place with his will alone. His familiars crowded round the Ravenmaster, circling like snarling, snapping wolves from some forgotten fairy tale.

Tristan felt as though he was encased in ice, and yet he mustered all his strength and gradually began to feel his muscles moving. He turned on the steps and looked down over Branok's head.

'You have miscalculated,' he growled, and the warlock turned to face him, a question written all over his face.

'Here you stand with your familiars gathered all about you, but who guards your precious bloodline now?' Tristan smiled.

Branok's eyes widened at the dawning realisation.

'What have you done?' he hissed.

'Scallywagging,' said Tristan, and reaching into his pocket he pulled out a single round of rifle ammunition. He tossed it, and Branok followed its passage through the air.

'No,' he reassured himself. 'Arthur would never allow it.'

'Assuming he was told,' snapped Gareth.

'Culpable deniability,' said Bors, cracking his knuckles.

'No!' Branok hissed. He turned and thrust out his hand to the west as though throwing a ball. Four of his familiars exchanged glances, burst into a sprint in that direction and jumped, launching their human forms into the air. No sooner were they off the ground than their bodies shrank into that of ravens, and they flew off in search of the members of the Royal Family.

'You cannot kill them all,' Branok shouted, desperate.

Tristan stretched and eased, feeling Branok's influence subsiding as his attention became divided.

'We can take out enough of them to make the monarchy an irrelevance, public opinion being what it is,' said Tristan, resting his blade across his shoulder.

Joseph and Daisy moved to bar the way between the knights and their master.

'Kill them,' Branok cried, and he ran for the gate.

Mordred threw Arthur off him, and the former king rolled across the floor, coming to a stop with his back against a table. Something fell to the floor beside him, clanging as it landed.

Mordred clambered to his feet and began landing kick after kick, directed at Arthur's head, but smashing into his arms instead, as he raised his arms to shield himself. Arthur cried out as he felt bones snap and splinter.

'Mordred,' he spluttered. 'Mordred, stop!'

To his relief, Mordred took a step back and stood, out of breath, regarding Arthur as he clambered to his feet.

'Why are you doing Branok's bidding?' he asked. 'What possible good can come of it?'

'An opportunity to take the chance that you once denied me,' said Mordred. 'I can inherit your crown. Lead. Rule.'

'Killing me won't help you! I have not been king since you felled me at Camlann!'

Mordred frowned.

'You fell?' he asked.

Arthur paused for a moment, realising that, of course, his son did not know; Mordred had died before him.

'What do you remember?' said Arthur.

Mordred drew Excalibur and pointed it towards Arthur.

'I remember this, slipping between my ribs. Your face fading with the light,' he said, his voice breaking. 'Killed by my own father.'

'But not before you killed him,' said Arthur. 'I died of my wounds, Mordred, when battle was done.'

Mordred stood in silence, still frowning, candlelight dancing across David Bolton's face.

'It can't be true,' said Mordred. 'Branok recalled me to overthrow you.'

'We died a millennium ago and more,' said Arthur, softly.

Mordred looked towards the door, in the direction Branok had fled.

'The ruling house is of a different bloodline now,' said Arthur, 'and Branok would do anything to protect it. That's why he brought you back, because he knew I would not stand idly by and allow him to attack the people. I have no standing in this land, beyond a silent stewardship which I share with my brethren below,' said Arthur.

'A deceit? An attempt to regain Excalibur?' said Mordred, unsheathing Excalibur once more. Arthur saw his arm shake. David Bolton's muscles were unaccustomed to such weight.

'Keep it,' said Arthur. 'It is but a sword, in a world where swords are the stuff of stories.'

He stepped forward. Mordred drew Excalibur back.

Arthur nodded towards the Colt.

'Look at what you have in your other hand. Look how I am dressed. Go up to the heights of this tower and look out upon the world you now inhabit. You will see I am telling the truth, son,' said Arthur. He beckoned towards the door.

'Any enmity between us can be put to rest in this new age,' Arthur concluded.

Mordred raised the revolver and pointed it at Arthur's chest.

Gareth brought his broadsword down vertically at Joseph's head, but the familiar was too fast and stepped aside. The weapon smashed into the ground, and the knight staggered forward with it. Joseph stepped up and drove his knee into Gareth's flank, cracking ribs. Gareth cried out and darted aside, stooping against the pain as he raised his sword once more, carving a divot from the lawn.

Tristan charged towards Branok, silent and deadly, he raised his sword above his head and when he was but a few yards away, he hurled it to the warlock's right. It narrowly missed Daisy, who ducked and kicked out, swiping Kay's legs from under him. She reached up as she did so and caught Tristan's sword.

Branok followed the path of the sword and was, momentarily, filled with relief as he saw Daisy stand and hack down with Tristan's sword, severing Kay's thigh. His scream echoed around the Tower.

Branok's world became a blur as something hit him with great force. Tristan had dived forward and driven his left forearm into Branok's throat. The knight and warlock flew backwards, with Tristan landing atop him. The knight fumbled in his coat, and Branok protested as Tristan pulled out a commando knife. The warlock reached out with his free hand and grabbed Tristan by the forehead, channelling all his strength through his fingertips. Tristan's eyes, normally a chestnut brown, drained of their colour until they were fully white. His tongue lolled from his mouth and a trail of saliva drooled out.

Bors kicked Branok's hand away, and Tristan slumped off to the side, shaking his head as he came back to the world.

The warlock grabbed Bors's foot and thrust it upwards so that he was off balance. Daisy burst into view and aimed wild swings with Tristan's sword at Bors's chest. He fell back, but the tip cut a gash across his chest.

Branok clambered to his feet, and when he turned he saw

Joseph snatch up Kay's sword and, standing side by side with Daisy, his familiars unleashed a fury upon the knights, unconstrained by a normal human body's limitations. It took all the men had just to fend off the blows, slipping in Kay's blood as he writhed on the ground beside them. A furious exchange of blows ensued, and Branok took the opportunity to once again run for the gate.

But Tristan was back on his feet, and now he called out to the warlock, levelling a Glock at the warlock's back.

Branok waved his hand, and a chasm shot forward, splitting the earth before Branok's feet and lancing forward between Tristan's legs towards the White Tower, throwing the knight off balance.

The split in the west wall of the White Tower widened, and the ground shook. Branok looked up as the stone began to crumble away.

And then he saw a lone figure standing atop the stairs.

Mordred ran down the steps, Excalibur in hand. He dashed past the melee of knights and familiars, ignoring Tristan who had been cast down and was clambering out of the narrow chasm which had opened up beneath him.

'Is it done?' cried Branok above the sound of splitting stone and rumbling earth, thunder booming overhead.

Mordred nodded.

'It soon will be,' he said and nodded back in the direction he had come.

Arthur stepped out from the White Tower. Branok's mouth fell open in a moment of sheer confusion, in which he could not comprehend any circumstances in which

Arthur and Mordred would allow one another to live, or in which Mordred might put aside his desire to be the king. Though Branok was a man who prized the handing down of nobility through blood above all else, he had forgotten the same might be true for this father and son.

He realised too late that he had made a mistake. As he did so, Excalibur's point burst through his chest and quivered in front of him. Mordred hauled the blade sideways, and Branok's insides were sliced through as he was tossed aside, his body thrown down upon the ground.

The warlock lay prone, and as blood trickled from his mouth, and he struggled to speak, he thrust out a finger towards Arthur, exerting what was left of his power, to no avail.

Mordred's spirit, bound to David Bolton's body through Branok's will in an unholy alliance, departed as the warlock died. David Bolton's corpse fell upon the lawn.

The battle ended in an instant as the familiars shrieked and imploded.

Arthur dashed down the steps as fast as his wounds allowed as the White Tower began to crumble and shake. The windows shattered and timbers gave way. The stones fell to rubble, laying the Tower's foundations bare, sending up a great cloud of dust.

A thousand ravens took to the skies as the White Tower fell.

But what of England?

Chapter Twenty-Five

February - 2020

'Well, he got what he wanted in the end,' said Tristan, folding his newspaper and throwing it down on the dining room table. It landed before Arthur with its headline clearly visible.

LONG LIVE THE QUEEN – UNITED KINGDOM BACKS ITS MONARCHY.

He nodded and lifted his mug of coffee to his lips, savouring the scent of it before drinking as he looked around the table at his surviving people, save for Agravain in prison and Bedivere, away on business.

'Aye, for now,' said Bors, 'but with the sickness, the rioting, the tremors and other mischief dying down, it won't be long before they start railing about the waste of public money and demanding the palaces are turned into libraries or housing for the homeless.'

Arthur set down his mug, seeing Bors shift as though ready to stand and be about his day.

'Wait a moment,' said Arthur. 'It's time to have the conversation we have all been avoiding.'

Bors settled in his seat once more. All of their expectant faces turned towards him.

Arthur thought of his fallen knights as he looked around the table, of Gaheris, Lamorak and Galahad, who fell at the Somme, of Geraint, who fell while the Great Fire of London raged and of Percival, the last to fall. And he thought of Merlin.

'I made you a promise,' said Arthur.

They said nothing, and so Arthur continued.

'Once, when we were but children, you heeded my words and followed me into battle, and I became king. Your king, king of a little land, still struggling to make its way in the world after the Romans left, dealing with the Norsemen and the Saxons. I was king for the blink of an eye, and then we rested and slept, duty done for a time.'

Tristan sat back in his chair, folding his arms across his chest.

'We were ripped from our rest and put back in that little land, finding it a changed place, beyond both our understanding and our reach, yet we have done what we could, and, in some small way, the prophecy was fulfilled.'

He looked around the table, making eye contact with each of his knights.

'But at what cost to our company? The silence in this room is a sound in itself, and none add to it more than do those who once sat upon the empty chairs,' he said, his words soft and sad and sorrowful. He raised his mug in a toast.

'To absent friends,' he said. The others reached for their own drinks and joined him in the toast, and Arthur knew that each of them felt the loss of a different companion the keenest.

'The time of service is over,' he said, and the words were stark to his own ears, ragged, a tattered banner flapping in the wind.

'I will not throw away a lifetime of duty,' said Tristan. 'My oath holds.'

'Gawain,' said Bors.

'We are a brotherhood,' said Gareth, and Dagonet nodded.

'And that will never change,' said Arthur. 'We are closer than brothers, and it is not right that I should be set apart on high any longer. Each of you has as much wisdom as do I, has seen this country change and quicken as the weary years rolled by. We have spilled much blood for Britain, and it is time that each of you took some joy for yourselves.'

He held up his hand to quieten Tristan before he could object further.

'I will not turn away from this decision,' said Arthur. 'It is done. You are all free to go where you wish and do as you desire. Carve out lives for yourselves. Love. Have families, if that is what your heart wants.'

He took up his coffee and sipped again.

'The company will continue our work, but we will not take up arms any longer. Let us enjoy this England. To that end, I have divided our funds amongst us, transferred it to each of your accounts equally. I will not turn you out into the cold as beggars,' said Arthur.

Tristan shook his head.

'This is not an end to friendship or brotherhood, nor am I dismissing you from this house or my company. But you are no longer beholden to me. And that is how true friendship should be,' said Arthur. 'How family should be.'

Silence.

Tristan sat scowling at Arthur, while Gawain could not raise his eyes from the surface of the table. Bors was clearly wrestling with some emotion that he could not articulate, and, quietly, as was his way, Dagonet spoke for them all, even if they did not realise it yet.

'Thank you, Arthur,' he said. And smiled.

All of them needed time to take a breath in private, and so Arthur retreated to his drawing-room. He built the fire, poured himself a brandy from a decanter and sat in his wingback chair, listening to the ticking of the clock and the crackling of the fire. Where once his arms from across the centuries had arrayed the walls, now there were mounted photographs of landscapes in black frames, his weapons donated or sold, all save for his Colt, secured in a gun safe.

His eyes settled on the empty chair on the other side of the fire, and he thought of Merlin. He sipped his brandy and indulged reminiscences of times gone by with the old man, who had been so much more than a mentor and a guide to him. Arthur drank to the wizard's memory.

In time, he drifted off to sleep, warmed by the fire.

When he awoke he found the house had a lazy Sunday

feel to it. The air was still, and one could believe that time made no progress on a day such as that.

Arthur pulled on his coat, gloves and boots, wrapped a scarf around his neck, grabbed his case and put on a wide-brimmed hat which he took from a hook behind the door. Arthur stopped to check his reflection in a mirror, and knew that his growing suspicion had been correct.

There were new wrinkles lining his forehead, marked crow's feet at the corners of his eyes, and he would need to buy a nose-trimmer, he decided, shaking his head in amusement. He did not know why he was ageing now, but suspected that his prolonged vigour had been Merlin's work. And with the wizard gone? It seemed in time he would once again have the release of death, and in some strange way, that comforted Arthur.

He snatched up a rifle case from where he had set it in the hall, and headed out into the snow to fetch the dogs. They wagged their tails and jumped up at him when he opened the doors. He stooped and fussed them for a moment until his leg cried out, and he straightened up, leaning on his cane.

'Come on then. Come on,' he said to them as he walked towards the gate, and the hounds bounded after and then ahead of him, so that he followed their trail of paw-prints in the snow.

His feet knew the way through this white landscape in which all features and points of reference were masked by ice and snow. Arthur walked slowly and noticed after a while that he was smiling while he did so, bundled up against the cold. The dogs led him across the road and into the trees, where he had to duck below branches until he found a deer path to follow.

Arthur stopped only when he reached the edge of a frozen pond at the centre of a small glade, surrounded by ancient oak trees, twisted and magnificent.

Arthur stood in silence. His breath escaped as clouds of vapour, and he smiled, remembering how he pretended to be a dragon as a child, scorching all around him.

The trees creaked overhead, the occasional twig snapped, and a branch fell in the middle distance. A squirrel ran up one of the oaks, and somewhere overhead, a buzzard mewed.

Arthur closed his eyes, searching inside his heart and mind. The decision was made.

He let his cane rest against his hip and used both hands to unzip the rifle case. From within it, he withdrew Excalibur, and held it aloft, admiring the craftsmanship and, in some way, yearning for the sword. He rested the blade across his gloved hand, and looked over the weapon from tip to pommel – the sword of the king, bound to the land.

Arthur stepped forward and cast Excalibur into the deep water at the centre of the pond.

Arthur had expected to feel regret after relinquishing the sword, but he felt lighter as he walked away from the pond, whistling to himself while the dogs trotted beside him, stopping only to sniff at hidden items or chase creatures on the path. He knew he had a world before him to explore, and the coming certainty of an end to his long days. He would bask in them, he decided, take pleasure in existing in the here and now. He would honour the past, but walk away from it.

His feet crunched the virgin snow as he walked down a sloping path between the trees until he stood before a thatched cottage. Lights twinkled in its windows and smoke billowed from its chimney pots that winter morning, ivy disguising its walls and a wooden gate before him with 'Hunter's Cottage' etched into the wooden crossbeam.

He pushed the gate open and walked up the path to knock three times, rapping on the wooden door with the head of his cane.

Arthur waited, almost patiently, wondering how he would be received, arriving unannounced. He heard nothing, not even Caitlyn's dog barking, and wondered if she was visiting family, or maybe working.

He sighed and departed, closing the gate behind him, and as he walked back up the path, he no longer whistled. And although his new life was still an edifying prospect, the excitement had diminished somewhat, as does the excitement of waking on Christmas morning with each year that passes.

But then Arthur saw Caitlyn ahead on the path, and she was smiling at the sight of him. His heart kindled once more.

'Good morning,' said Caitlyn.

'I was walking the dogs, and I thought I'd stop by,' he said. 'I hope you don't mind.'

His face flushed, and he wondered if the snowflakes would sizzle as they touched his skin.

'Don't be silly,' she said, and she took him to her in an embrace, just briefly, but with a little squeeze that shortened his breath. Her perfume ignited his senses, and he smiled fully as they drew apart.

'Have you got time for a hot chocolate?' she asked, pushing the gate to her home slightly open, and Arthur pushed it the rest of the way.

'All the time in the world,' he said.

Please leave a review if you enjoyed the book!

The story continues in *Agravain's Escape: The Return of King Arthur*. Find out more here: www.jacobsannox.com/agravains-escape.html

If you haven't already, sign up to the Jacob Sannox Readers' Club newsletter, and you will receive a free copy of the first book of my epic fantasy series, **The Dark Oak Chronicles**; a semi-finalist in the 2018 SPFBO competition. I will also keep you updated about new releases, giveaways and discounts. It will not cost you anything, you won't receive any spam, and you can unsubscribe at any time - www.jacobsannox.com/darkoakfree.html

Printed in Great Britain
by Amazon

45476039R00135